AWKWARD STAGES

A Book of Short Stories

Mark Victor Young

Awkward Stages

Copyright

Awkward Stages: A Book of Short Stories by Mark Victor Young

Published by **Hanton House Creative Media** in London, Ontario, Canada.

First print edition March 2015

ISBN: 978-0-9938558-4-9

Enquiries: HHCreativeMedia@icloud.com

Cover Designed by Christina Young at http://christinalorraineyoung.com/

For any reuse or distribution, you must make clear to others the license terms of this work. The best way to do this is with a link: http://markvictoryoung.com/

More info about Creative Commons here: http://creativecommons.org

For Christina, as always.

Awkward Stages

Introduction

First of all, thanks for buying this book. With all the competing media out there working to capture your time and attention these days, I appreciate anyone who takes the time to read a book for enjoyment. If a boring introduction makes you want to put a book down and switch on the TV, you can just skip ahead.

Writing short stories was one of the ways I found my voice as a writer. They were a great way to experiment with ways of expressing myself, to wrestle with the narrative ideas I had, and later to develop others that weren't quite a novel, but still something which needed a medium. Early in my career as a writer, I constantly sent out short stories and poems to various literary journals. Those interactions with editors and occasional offers of publication were vital to my development as a writer. They let me know I was on the right path or helped me change direction when I needed to.

Later in my career, those lit mags turned into online literary websites, but getting an occasional win from an editor is just as important now as it was then. The stories in this collection were selected to represent the best of the best of my career in short fiction. They are in an order which makes sense to me, but this makes it a thematic retrospective, I guess, and not a chronological one.

At the end of the book you'll find the first chapters of some of my novels as well as the first short story in a new collection currently under development which deals with the ex-pat crowd in 1920's Paris.

When you've finished this book, I'd love for you to share your comments or a short review wherever you purchased it. If you enjoyed it or are enticed by one of the samples at the end, I hope you'll consider purchasing one of my other books down the road.

Mark Victor Young
London, Canada
March 2015

Crotch Dogs

My best friend in Grade Nine was a girl, but we weren't boyfriend and girlfriend; our relationship was purely platonic. Katy was interested in all the best stuff. She loved Star Wars movies and comics and role-playing games—even more than I did—and she was the smartest person I knew. We always ended up at her house after school, watching TV, reading books or just talking in her basement, trying to avoid her "Little Bother." She had two enormous Pyrenees Mountain Dogs who would jam their sniffers right into your crotch area as soon as you walked in, but they were mostly harmless as long as you didn't get knocked over and licked to death.

We went to the same public school and met in the library during the last half of Grade Eight. We were in different classes, but both of us volunteered as library helpers. I did it mostly to avoid being picked on at recess, but Katy seemed to want to read the entire library. She volunteered so she could get to know the books she wanted to read next. So we shelved together and hung out in the stacks and she would tell me one of her amazing theories about the Way Things Are or

9

some story about her *Hero de Jour,* like the time Plato got in trouble with the King of Syracuse and got sold into slavery for a while until a wealthy admirer paid for his freedom and he returned to spreading his wisdom across the land. Good times.

The summer after Grade Eight I spent a lot of time over at her house, often reading from book lists she prepared for me. We rode our bikes, swam in her pool, went to movies, fended off her dogs and just hung out. Neither of us had a summer job and her parents both worked, so we pretty much had the run of the place, although we had to look after her brother, Davey. She would pick a topic for us to research and then we would spend part of the day at the public library reading everything we could about it, making notations in these little spiral-bound notebooks her mom got us. By the end of the day, we would be smarter than anyone else in the world about Roman mythology, African tree frogs or some former Canadian Prime Minister. Or so we thought at the time.

It might seem as though that would be boring, but Katy made it seem really challenging and interesting, like a murder mystery we were solving. She would get right into it, her brown hair hanging in a curtain in front of her face as she concentrated, her skinny arms hugging a book on one side and scribbling with a pen on the other as she made notes. She had a kind of freckly face and a nice smile, good teeth (which meant no braces, unlike me) and dark eyes. The goal of all that studying was to totally victimize our teachers with trivial minutiae when those topics came up in class. It felt good to know more about something than a grown-up. And to think it was all just waiting for us at the library whenever we felt like knowing something.

Of course, Davey was too little to stay at home alone, so we had to take him with us to the library all the time. The three of us would bike down there together with our backpacks full of books to be returned and come home later with another full load. He would always play with the train sets or watch a video while we were into our research and then he would get a big bunch of dinosaur books to take out. He was into dinos in a big way. He was always playing with toy dinos, reading dino books, getting his mom to take him to "The Land Before Time" twelve times that summer and he also went to a Dinosaur-themed day camp at the museum for one week. He would come screaming into Katy's room, flapping his arms and she would say, "Get out of here, Pteranadon. There are no scrumptious jubjubs in here for you." And out he would go, still screaming and cawing like mad.

Katy's theory about why all kids seemed to go through a phase about dinosaurs was that it's their first hint regarding their own mortality. I'll call this the Dinosaur Theory.

"The existence of dinosaurs," she said. "Is the first frightening concept for a child because they are evidence of the possibility of extinction, of which the child has never before conceived. Because dinosaurs are extinct, it means that things die. Even kids. What force fueled their inability to survive—was it random or deliberate? How will Death come for us and is it something we should watch out for? Will it come when we are dreaming and is that something which should keep us awake at night? These questions are part of the fear and fascination kids have with dinosaurs."

"Huh," I said. "It's not just because they were totally powerful and cool? Like with wicked claws and teeth and stuff?"

"Sure. That's part of it, too."

"Okay, I was going to say."

The summer passed quickly, as all summers do. The specter of high school loomed large in my imagination. I envisioned a lawless place where an innocent "Niner" could run afoul of the pack in a single misjudged reaction or statement and be stuffed in a locker, given a swirly or any other form of torture dreamed up by seniors, juniors or your former friends from public school. But at least I had one friend on my side and if we could manage to avoid notice, it was at least possible that we could survive for the entire year in the library. Katy didn't seem worried, which gave me confidence.

The social scene at our high school, when the day finally came that we were dropped into that thick soup of posturing and insecurity, included all the usual cliques: the jocks, the nerds, the student council, the preppies, the rampers, the stoners, the losers, the debate club freaks and the band geeks. And then there were the legendary In-Betweeners: those who skirted the edges of other group concerns without getting sucked in to all the hoopla. The key to this very select group was ironic detachment. We were too cool to belong.

But in all the groups there were the hormone cases. One girl and one guy who came together like all the magnets in science class suddenly clamped on to each other in a desperate lip lock of primal urges. The whole school was filled with these kinds of barely concealed gropings and snoggings in the hallways and by open lockers. Like Katy's dogs, they were sniffing at each other's crotches and even, it seemed, humping legs. It was really kind of sick. There was a reason we were above all that and that reason was Plato.

"Is this our fate?" said Katy. "To be such slaves to our animal instincts, our genetic predilections? Must we have this constant reminder of our Neanderthal lineage? This dirty, sweaty sex thing always controlling our every move? Will we never evolve to the Platonic Ideal of Love? If only we could find a comfortable way of surgically removing the urge, what a difference it would make to the world."

"Well, it would certainly curb the over-population issue," I said.

"Exactly," she said. "A great peripheral benefit."

"So nobody would fall in love anymore?"

"There would be more love, not less. Just not romantic love."

I loved the feeling of certainty she always had, the sense that she had everything figured out. When my parents were going through a horrible divorce during my first couple of years in high school, she was a comforting distraction. Even if I had a tendency towards certain feelings, or longings shall we say, regarding her, her certainty about the higher beauty of Platonic Love kept me at bay. I'll call this the Love Theory.

"There is no logical argument which can prove the existence of love," she said. "It's a leap of faith. To non-believers, love is nothing but a crossed wire between sentiment and sexual desire. Sentiment itself is simply a survival instinct connected to the time when a mother's protection meant safety. All emotions, therefore, are based on explainable chemical reactions in the brain.

"But for those of us who believe in love, there is no

higher form of it than Platonic Love. It is love freed from the chains of sexual desire and possessiveness. It is a recognition of the beauty we see in others as it is connected to the source of all beauty and divinity in the world."

"So no marriage and babies," I said. "I get that. But wasn't Plato gay anyway? It kind of makes sense he wouldn't be interested in those things."

"Unproven," she said. "The ancient Greeks spoke of love in different ways, so we just might not understand their references to love between men."

"But he never got married."

"No."

"And that was because he didn't believe in Romantic Love?"

"Yes, that's what I believe."

"Okay," I said. "But he had this 'Allegory of the Cave,' right? Which I don't really get, by the way, but anyway. It's all about the things in our world being just shadows on the wall of a cave, cast by a flickering fire light. How is he going to see the shadow of love up on the wall?"

"That's just it. For Plato, love didn't have a physical form. It was spiritual."

"Okaaaaaay. It just seems more like the love that dare not speak its name."

"Get your mind out of the gutter and you'll understand Plato," she said.

"We are all in the gutter," I said. "But some of us are looking at the stars. Oscar Wilde."

Of course, I never really said this, but I wish that I had. All of my profundity was of the kind that I imagined and inserted years later into our remembered conversations. Maybe some of hers, too. I know I felt

14

like a clumsy oaf around her much of the time, led around by the ear by her genius. It was enough to me that she believed something to believe in it myself. So Platonic Love it was, but the pressing urgencies of adolescence were not to be denied. When an embarrassing erection makes a tent of the front of your rugby pants in the hallway of your high school, it's difficult not to believe in it.

So it was a surprise to hear that Katy wanted to go to the first high school dance that year. What other reason was there for dancing than the search for that tawdry, pre-dawning of the Age of Aquarius compulsion called Romantic Love? We rolled up at the front door of our school at 7:30 on a Friday night, paid our $2.00 admission to the Student Council and we were in. The halls were lined with teachers posted as Sentries Against Funny Business. It felt weird to be in the school at night and I wondered why the teachers would want to spend their night at the place where they worked all day just so a bunch of kids could dance in the gym. Nice of them. They didn't even look too miserable, smiling at us as we walked past.

There were some kids sitting and talking in the cafeteria and in the hallway and we could already hear the loud noise coming from the gym ahead of us, which was dark. There was a teacher I didn't know in the doorway with his back to us as we walked in and felt the full force of the music and all the dim colored lights pointing at the half-hearted decorating job the social committee made of the walls and ceiling. It was a fast song, so people were cavorting in little groups all around the dance floor and there were others loitering near the outside wall, whisper shouting at each other.

"Look at all the sniffing and humping going on in

here," I shouted in Katy's ear. "It's a whole room full of Crotch Dogs."

"Yeah," said Katy. She was looking around at everything, seemingly distracted and lost in her own thoughts.

"I'm just going to the bathroom," I shouted.

"Okay," she shouted back.

I left her by the locker room doors, still taking it all in. I passed clusters of boys and clusters of girls on my way to the bathroom, each cluster sizing up the other for signs of movement. Would one individual emerge from the group and make the brave trek across the six feet which separated them to risk rejection in the most public, humiliating form? Like a red crossing the roulette wheel to put all its money on black, while the whole room kept on spinning.

It was a relief to emerge from the dark gym into the slightly quieter hallway, which was bright with fluorescents. I saw my English teacher standing and talking to a couple of boys I didn't know, so I waved at her and kept going. I entered the bathroom to the sound of someone saying "Bleah" really loudly. It was as though someone asked him if he liked mushroom soup and he showed his disdain by saying, "Bleah." But when I rounded the corner to see fully into the room, I could see a boy kneeling on the floor, puking into a backpack. Three other boys were there with him, laughing and high-fiving, pushing each other into the sinks. The acid vomit stench hit me and I just looked straight ahead and crossed the floor to an empty stall, pulling the door closed behind me.

Standing there, having my private pee, I considered what the heck I was doing there. At the dance and really in my life in general. Was I just going to trail along behind Katy as she made notes for her future anthropological thesis? A harmless minion? A subservient admirer? Or was I going to say what I'd wanted to for a long time, but couldn't ever quite find the words to say? Was it going to come out as an approximation of "I'd like to clasp your sweaty body quite close to mine and shuffle in circles in the dark?" How is that any different from all the other knuckleheads out there, or this guy in the bathroom, letting go of a stomachful of barley, hops and pizza? I needed an angle to come at this thing which she would respect.

I zipped up with a vague idea that I would ask her to dance in the tradition of courtly love. "Prithee fair lady, gentle friend, wilt thou dance with this base knave?" Something like that. It couldn't be helped that I didn't actually know any ancient dances of court and we'd really just be shuffling in circles. I opened the stall door to find the boys were all gone and, strangely, so was the backpack. I washed my hands and appraised my face in the mirror. Dork. Metal Mouth. Pimply and pale with prominent, swollen-looking features. Greasy hair because I was on a Day Two of my shower schedule. At least it wasn't a dreaded Day Three when I couldn't pull myself out of bed in the morning. Why couldn't the dance have fallen on a glorious Day One when my hair did that neat feathering out to the sides thing?

If I'd had some notice that we were planning to go to the dance, I could've snapped into action and done a back-to-back shower that morning with just one suds instead of two. But there we were at our lockers, getting ready to go home after last class and she just all of a sudden came out with this crazy plan.

"It will be like a social experiment," she said. "We

17

will be there as observers, as anthropologists noting the mating habits of the urban teenager."

"Well, that sounds like fun," I said. "Will we be carrying binoculars and notebooks? Because that won't look geeky and get me beat up at all."

"You'll be fine," she said. "We'll just blend in with the crowd and see what happens."

Despite my disappointing appearance and a persistent fear of ending up head first in a garbage can, I left the bathroom resolved to ask her to dance. I figured I'd lay down a little Middle English on her: "Little wot it any mon, how derne love may stonde. But it were a free wymmon, that much of love had fonde." I think that's how it went. It would be that much better if I could bust out a few Medieval or Renaissance dance moves to go with it. I went back to the spot in the gym by the locker room doors where I had left her, but she was nowhere around there. I looked up and down the gym walls to see if she might be talking to somebody she knew, but no luck there, either.

I decided she must have also gone to the washroom, so I found an out of the way place to wait. I was just scanning the pairs on the floor who were dancing to a slow song when I realized that Katy was in one of those couplings. She was dancing with some tall guy. As I waited for them to make their slow rotation around so I could see his face, I noticed to my shock and horror that they weren't just dancing, they were literally sucking on each other's faces. How had this happened? How could she be doing that? With him? Where should I stand and what do I do with my hands in this situation? I shifted my weight first onto one foot, then the other. I turned to leave the gym and then turned back, frozen to the wall, feeling a sense of the

"Bleah" rising in my own stomach. Where could I get out of this noise, this damn twirling disco light?

Katy didn't seem to notice me and what was worse, she didn't look at all out of place dancing with the captain of the basketball jock asshole squad, her hair flipped back off her forehead in a cute way, her training bra small chest poking out at him and the jeans which looked normal when we were on our way here looking all of a sudden very form-fitting, her skinny legs seeming more like what you'd call slim and when did her hips start curving out like that? And since when had there been Platonic tonsil hockey, for Christ's sake? How could Katy be a Crotch Dog? She invented the term. That was it... I was so done with Plato.

That moment up against the wall, feeling sick and betrayed, was the instant end of my romantic feelings for Katy, although we remained best friends throughout the remainder of our high school years and to this day. Suffice it to say that I took her wonderful Theories with a grain of salt after that. And came up with a few of my own. Like the one where Oscar Wilde kicks Plato's ass any day of the week and twice on Sundays.

Awkward Stages

Fault Lines

We were going to a party up in the North End—
somebody's basement, probably. First we had to stop
by Ed's house. He's the one who called Barney with
the plan in the first place. Before that, I think we had
planned to get some grape pop and barbecue chips and
play video games, but then Ed called.

"It's on. I heard about this epic party tonight," he
said. "Swing by and we'll catch the bus together."

So we swung by. Ed was still getting ready, so we sat
and chatted with his mom in the living room. I could
smell the soapy humidity from his recent shower and
the copious amounts of CK One he had sprayed on his
person from my seat on the couch. He was humming to
himself, which was adorable. There was also a low
background noise of sports on TV coming from the
basement.

"So," said Ed's mom. "Do you boys have any classes
with Edward?"

I shrugged and Barney went ahead with a long
explanation of the many fascinating subjects and
inspiring educators for whom both he and her son

21

shared a scholarly affection and a coincidental schedule overlap. Barney was better with parents, although not as good as Ed. I looked around the living room and tried to imagine someone choosing this furniture at a store and paying money for the right to have it in their home.

What was fun about this? Mrs. Lipski and her sad Saturday night. Mr. Lipski with a beer in one hand and the remote in the other. Both of them with kids and responsibilities and this god awful furniture to pay for. Five long, cruel workday grinds a gunk in their psyche they can't shake loose. Yet the onward momentum of time is constantly dragging everybody into this early end called adulthood, like some dark hood that covers over your head, shrouding your ears, pulling tight in the front and obscuring all features as it cinches closed around most of your face and you can't even tell who a person is anymore.

Then Ed came down. He looked good. He smelled of body wash and way too much cologne and his hair wasn't completely dry, which put a constriction on my chest right around my rib cage like a belt that went one hole too far. His smile was optimism and enthusiasm and confidence.

"You guys ready?" he said.

"Yes," I said and stood up.

Ed got his boots and coat on and said goodbye to his mom and led us out the front door, down the steps and around the path to the back of the house where he had two green bottles hidden under a bush in the snow. There were two big, grape-y stickers with the words "White/Blanc" in an ornate script.

"Very fancy, monsieur," said Barney. He took one from Ed before he could put it in his backpack. "The

U-brew special. Won't your dad miss these prize vintages from his collection?"

"The vintage is last Tuesday," said Ed. "And he's got cases of the stuff in the basement."

"Well, it's very chilled," said Barney. "How long has it been out here?"

"Ever since my dad went to Canadian Tire this afternoon and my mom took a shower."

"A proud tradition for any Canadian," said Barney. He passed the bottle back to Ed to put in the backpack with the other. Ed slung one strap over his right shoulder and we walked single file back along the path and through his driveway to the street. Once we were on the bus, Ed told us how it would be.

"Gentlemen," he said. "This party will be so awesome."

"Tell us, Obi-wan," said Barney.

"I've heard there will be six kegs. It's going to be sick. And the place will be just crawling with pussy."

I laughed at this mental image.

"I'm serious," said Ed. "If you can't get laid at this party, you're not really trying."

"Right on," said Barney.

I looked at the huge smiles on both their faces as they high-fived and the two wine bottles clinked from within the backpack. We all laughed and I imagined the boners they were sporting inside their jeans and wished them luck, I guess. I half listened to their banter on the rest of the journey as the bus doors opened and closed, hissed and dinged, and we were jostled over every bump and pothole along the icy hills and snowy streets.

The party was lame. It was in somebody's basement, as I had thought it would be, and there was exactly zero kegs. The guy's mom had bought all new furniture, so nobody was allowed in the living room. The rumors of a large feline contingent were comically incorrect. One guy had brought his girlfriend and she looked understandably uncomfortable around the entirely canine group of drunk, horny guys. They left early and this one guy took acid so somebody put on some trippy Pink Floyd music. Woopdie fucking woop.

The white wine was both acidic and sweet. We drank it straight from the bottle in order to make the sad basement seem more entertaining. It was crowded with old furniture—probably the set that got bumped by Mrs. Whatever's new stuff upstairs. I couldn't help thinking that the grape pop and the Doritos with the video games would have been more fun. The three of us like to keep up a trash-talking commentary about our avatars in the game world and mess with the guy who dies first. Barney, usually. Ed and I made the better team.

Things got real and they got hard during what came next and we came to rely on Ed's gamesmanship more than ever. The party fizzled, and then collapsed in on itself. Someone put on a grainy porno for a while, which caused stretches of silence but for the phony moaning coming from the old television set, alternating with loud cat calls and whooping bravado in that room full of mostly drunk virgins. The sound (and smell) of someone puking reached us from the downstairs bathroom. The evening was over before it began. People started leaving in ones and twos. It was getting close to midnight and the last bus.

We walked out into the cold night air in this strange neighborhood in the North end and tried to lurch and stumble our way back along the roads we'd come in on, laughing loudly at nothing.

"We didn't go this way," said Barney.

Ed laughed and pushed him in the shoulder. "It's a shortcut."

"You don't know," said Barney, which made me giggle.

As we passed one side street I could see a school in the distance and a large group of boys coming through the gate of the schoolyard towards us. A couple of them had baseball bats, but it was pretty late to be playing ball, I thought to myself, and then I was sober.

"Guys," I said. "We need to get to that bus stop expeditiously."

Ed turned and looked at me with a lazy smile, but when he looked where I inclined my head and saw what I had seen, he was right away sober, too. The group of boys was about a hundred yards away from us, but picked up speed perceptibly when they rounded the corner of the side street and came our way.

"Hey, guys," someone shouted. "Wait up." Laughter.

"Okay," Ed said to us. "Walk fast but don't run."

"Yes," I said to him. "But to where are we walking fast? I really don't remember coming this way."

"We'll go straight ahead to the stop sign and I think we'll see Wonderland Road to our left."

Barney looked back over his shoulder and gulped audibly. Perhaps it was a nervous belch. We kept up our pace and I, too, took a look back over my shoulder. They had gained ground on us. Probably seventy yards away and laughing in a cruel way and making inaudible comments to each other.

"Hey, fags," somebody yelled from behind us.

"We're talking to you. Where are you lover boys off to?"

What the fuck? How'd we go there all of a sudden?

"Just keep walking," said Ed.

The stop sign was about twenty paces away. It was a T-intersection and it didn't look familiar to me. The gang behind us was about fifty yards away now and closing fast, shouting epithets relating to cowardice, homosexuality, intellectual simplicity and other projected shortcomings. As we came to the end of the street, I could see down to the left. There was another stop sign in the distance which wasn't Wonderland. Off to the right, the road simply curved away out of sight. Damn these complicated suburban grid plans!

"Left," said Ed, and it was then that the mob began to run after us, so we ran across the lawn of the house on the corner. They were howling and cat-calling like a pack of wild dogs. I could feel my heart muscle gearing me up for fight or flight and a sparking mix of chemicals coming from my adrenal gland was encouraging me towards the former. I wanted to do some damage on these hooligans, give them a surprise when the hunted swiftly turns on the hunters and bares his fangs. But I followed Ed at a full run, up a driveway and onto the front porch of the house there.

"What are we doing?" I said.

"Where is this?" said Barney, who had joined us on the porch and turned around to keep an eye on the pack behind us. I turned to see if they were scaling the steps on our heels, but they had subsided around the front of the lawn and were taunting us from the edge of the driveway. I heard Ed ring the doorbell. The white wine was like a lake of fire in me.

I breathed in and out and Barney and I traded

glances. There was fear in his eyes. I never thought there would be roving gangs in North London. The East End, yes, but this was unexpected. This made our situation all the more uncomfortable, because it was difficult to gauge what they were capable of doing to us. How far would they take this? The porch light came on and the door opened.

A lady in a big purple sweater and polyester-looking tan pants was standing there looking out at us. She looked sleepy and confused. Our savior! Her marmalade tabby cat put her front paws up on the screen door window and peered out at us.

"Good evening, ma'am," said Ed. "Thank-you so much for opening the door. You see, my friends and I are in a bit of a situation. We're not from this neighborhood and we got lost on our way to the bus and attracted the attention of this group of boys who seem to want to do us harm."

The lady clicked the lock on her screen door. "Well, you can't come in here," she said.

"No, no," said Ed. "I wouldn't even ask you that favor. But I was wondering if you could call us a cab. We'll just wait here on your porch and then be out of your hair."

Barney and I both turned to see what her response would be. She looked at Ed, then me, then Barney, then out at the crowd of boys at the end of her driveway. "Tommy McIntyre," she said under her breath. At least, that's what I heard. "Just a second." She shooed the cat out of the way and then closed and locked her front door.

We all turned to look at the mob. They sneered and jeered at us. Barney, whose full name was James Robert Irving Barnett, was breathing so hard it started to sound more like a wheeze or a whimper.

"I'd like to see just one of these guys come at me and offer up a fair fight," I said. "They're really brave when they outnumber us ten to one."

"That's the whole point," said Ed.

"What, that they're a bunch of pussies?"

"Shh," said Ed.

The door clicked and then opened behind us and we turned around to face the cat lady.

"A cab is on its way," she said.

"Thank-you so much, ma'am," said Ed. "We really appreciate it."

"You're welcome," she said. "I can't believe this gang of punks is out at this hour giving you trouble. This used to be such a nice neighborhood. Tch."

I thought of the dormant game systems sitting in my basement, the grape pop chilling in the fridge, the barbecue chips and the perfect freshness seal of the foil bag, the peanut M&Ms that might have rewarded the winners of each game. Why had it been necessary to come out into this? In search of what? It felt like a punishment of some sort.

Ed and Barney and I had been friends since grade school. Our houses formed a triangle surrounding the public school we used to go to, all within a stone's throw of one of the gates into the yard. We played on the climbers or around the batting cage or just out on the tarmac till after dark on countless nights. The question, "What are you doing this weekend?" didn't even need to be asked. We would be getting together. That was automatic. Someone would come up with something—usually Ed—and we'd do it. Compadres, or amigos, was what we were.

It wasn't often we questioned each other, but Barney

and I had been out of our element at that party and Ed
wasn't. It was like a foreknowledge of a coming
tectonic plate shift. It wasn't a question of "if," it was a
question of "when?" The resulting shake up would be
irrevocable. Ed and his beautiful jawline and cowlick
hair were bound for a different social scene. A different
strata. Barney and I were grape pop and Ed was white
wine. Or some other fermented product, stimulant,
bullshit, bravado, popularity in a pill.

And even there, the sex thing was a fault line in the
whole strata for me—a diastrophism which would
essentially separate me from my friends. There would
never be a party at which Ed and I would have too
many drinks and spend too much time talking and then
he would be kind of looking at me in a certain way and
then take my face in his hands and kiss me. It wasn't
going to happen, as much as I might want or hope for
it. I knew it, just like I knew Barney and I would stay
video game friends forever and I would listen to his
thoughts on girlfriends and school dances and who he
liked but why she would never like him. For some
reason, the pain of these realizations in that moment
was worse than the fear and adrenaline I was feeling
due to our shitty situation.

I watched Ed talking to the cat lady through the
screen door and looked back at Barney, who was
chewing his cuticles, and then out at the group of idiots
still waiting for us at the end of the driveway. What
was the point of it all? There was no high score or level
up waiting at the end of this night for anyone.

A cab pulled up to the stop sign at the T-intersection,
and then turned into the driveway. The sea of boys
parted to let it through, beginning to renew their
laughing and jeering. We were fags and losers and we

could go fuck ourselves. On some level—deep inside their lizard brains—they probably thought that they had bravely defended their turf. The cab flashed its lights at us and we thanked the cat lady and went home.

The Tree House

From a prone position on the deck, Hugh eyed the pool: it was blue like the sky, which poured down sunlight into the million refracting beads of its captive fluid atmosphere. The surface of the water morphed and undulated like a drunken mirror. The diving board's reflection appeared to be chewing, perhaps on some gristle of a diver's foot, which it seemed prepared to spit into the pool. Squashed against the fence, behind the pool and beside the apple tree with the tree house, was the vegetable garden which he was to water on the off day unless it rained in which case he should seed the lawn. Hugh grunted in boredom and picked up his cell phone.

Pressing lazily against each of the ten required buttons, Hugh tipped back the last of his beer and set the bottle down on the table. This was his first vacation away from the vacation—he had been allowed to stay at home alone. His parents and younger brother Joshua were far off in cottage country, probably complaining about mosquitoes, the cold water, or their sleeping quarters. That's what cottage vacations were all about.

"Hello?"

"Hi, Joel."

"Hey, Hugh… How's life as a free man?"

"Not bad."

"Has she called you?"

"Who?" said Hugh.

"Robin."

"Oh. No. I thought you meant about graduation. How'd you find out about Robin?"

"Christie told me. I guess Robin's pretty mad. What'd you say to her?"

"I dunno. Just said I didn't want to see her anymore."

"You didn't give any reason?"

"No."

"Dude, do you even know what she's going to do to you on Facebook?"

"Yeah. I took my Facebook page down."

"You went off the air completely?" said Joel.

Hugh could picture his exact expression as he was saying this on the other end of the phone. Squinty eyes and stuff. "Yeah, I had Facebook fatigue, anyway. I'm sure nobody does that shit in college."

"Sure, right. Nobody. So why did you?"

"What?"

"Break up with her."

"What do you care?"

"Just why."

"Why is it's her fault. And you can tell her that… God knows she'll hear it, anyway. She's the one that's moving halfway across the planet. What am I supposed to think, that we have a future? Gimme a break."

"Hey, if I got into Berkeley I'd go, too. What's the big deal? School only lasts eight months and she'll be home for Christmas. Christie's going away, too, you know."

"So what? That's your problem."

"Geez, get an attitude, buddy."

"Yeah, yeah. What'cha doin' tonight? Want to come over?"

"Nah, me and Christie are going to the movies with Eric and his girlfriend from Toronto. You can come with, if you want."

"Naw, I'll skip it. Give me a call tomorrow."

"Okay, bye."

He got up out of his chaise longue and did a few of his usual pre-game stretches in the sun. He climbed the wooden porch steps, opened the patio door, shuffled his bare feet across the soft carpeted floor, then along the cool linoleum in the climate-controlled air to the kitchen. The whole house smelled of the burgers he had cooked for lunch. He opened the fridge, the cool blast made twice as cold by the relative heat of his body. There was a bowl of some leftover butternut squash soup, so he peeled back the plastic wrap, stuck in his finger and licked it.

Western University had accepted his request for fall admission into the Engineering program. He did not know why he should be pleased by this prospect of four more years of school, but his parents had been. Engineering was so job-related... it felt like practical training for a real job. But at least he had the summer.

Robin had been his girlfriend for three years, his first. It felt strange to be without her. It used to be a whole group of them, seven or eight anyway, and nobody was really "with" anybody on any given day. Then one time, he was feeling bummed about a big fight he'd had with his dad that day about having a curfew and she hung back a little from the crowd and asked him what the matter was and he said nothing, but the way she laughed made him think she knew he was lying and she put her arm around him and her hair smelled good and it was kind of the two of them after that. But that was all over, and he'd never asked to be part of a couple, anyway. It just sort of happened.

The break-up had been a dignity-preserving maneuver. Offense is the best defense. Because she would be moving away at the beginning of September, he had expected that she would request that they "not see each other for awhile." Considering that this would be impossible to avoid, anyway, he merely made it official; he struck the first blow instead of receiving it. Eric and Julia, Joel and Christie, Gord and whoever that chick was from New Year's... how many of them would still be together by the end of university? And what does it matter, anyway?

September: the single word like a punitive sentence. July, meanwhile, was hot.

He wandered out into the heat again, briefly considered and abandoned the idea of a swim, and then sauntered over to his brother's tree house as if he had nothing better to do. His father had built it for Josh two years ago and Hugh was forbidden to enter it, just as Josh was forbidden entry into Hugh's bedroom. Secrecy is a very important aspect of independence. The tree house was a private world, uninvaded by adult surveillance. A small, grimy window pane obscured the interior of the wooden tree-shanty and made its contents all the more mysterious. Hugh grabbed the lowest branch and hoisted himself up.

Once inside, he had to sit down with his knees hugged to his chest to compact his oversize body. The thin planks had formed a square-like floor plan, closer to a parallelogram, as the crux of the huge apple tree had dictated. The world beyond was a mixture of vague impressions as he peered out through the smeared glass—dull green globes hung from jagged brown wires, a flat expanse of green sprouted a gray face with blank square eyes framed by white trim, a glowing blue rectangle sparkled in a flat graph paper grid of white squares and a wall of beige contained them all.

Inside the small space, it was an even hotter July than the one over by the pool. There was a single raised plank for a chair and a box which bore the painted description: "Josh's Treasure Box." Hugh huddled his weight onto the plank and surprisingly, it did not break. He held the treasure box in his hands and ran his fingers over the smooth lid, feeling the ridges of the dry, painted words. In the box were the secrets which defined Joshua's private person. To look in it would be an invasion. He smiled at this foolishness and opened the lid.

There was a jumble of disparate items, which he pulled out and examined one by one: two comic books, twelve assorted bottle caps, the Teenage Mutant Ninja Turtle Josh had received for his birthday in April, a broken water pistol, a spent plastic shotgun shell (he had one just like it from hunting with their uncle—they were allowed to carry the empty leather satchel over one shoulder and their uncle scared rabbits with the horribly loud noise of the gun), sixteen plastic soldiers, a G.I. Joe figure with one leg, two cat's eye marbles, a beer bottle with no label, and an opened condom with a pine cone in it. This last one made him laugh.

He placed each item on the floor carefully and when he had finished, he put them all back in the box. He remembered owning such things when he was ten. Then he closed the lid and dusted it off with the palm of his hand. "Josh's Treasure Box," it said. It was a time capsule; a point in a life captured in perfection.

Somewhere inside the house the phone started ringing and he just sat there and let it continue like the bleating of an electronic sheep.

The Practical Uses of Voodoo in the Workplace

Monday

Beth was going to South Korea to teach ESL and Sandra who pronounced it Sohndrah was pregnant. This was the news that was waiting for office slave Patric Zulli on his first day back from vacation. As a result, his first coffee of the day was one tinged with bitterness, although it might just have been that he had lost some of his tolerance for the extra burnt flavor produced by the office's Brew Rite 5000 coffee maker.

It felt like Beth was just finished her training and finally getting her work done in a timely fashion and now it was going to begin all over again with someone new. Sandra had a belly time-bomb shelf life of five and a half months, so maybe the new Beth would be hired and trained just as they had to cover for Sandra's Mat leave as well. That would last a year. Their team would be down one person for a year and a half. And how was your vacation, Patric?

Patric felt in his pocket for the small wooden box of

37

Guatemalan worry dolls he had bought as a souvenir on his trip to the old country. Fitting two of the dozen into a large paper clip, then pinning them to the side of his cubicle wall, he took a sip of coffee while thinking up an appropriate voodoo incantation. *With these trombone clips I thee restrain; attempts to leave me shall be in vain.* This brought a smile to his face as he put the wooden box away under the pen tray in the top drawer of his desk.

He closed the drawer on his supplies for the time being, switching on his computer and casting a look in the direction of the boss lady Catherine's cubicle. The megacube. It looked out over their department, which was in a rectangular grid with four cubicles on each side and a common area in the middle around a table and four chairs for impromptu brainstorming sessions that never happened. The only thing that ever went on that table was the mail and a box of donuts every treat day. Patric shared a wall with Sandra, his cube buddy, oh bliss.

The octuplets, as he called the members of his department, faced the forbidding wall of Fortress Catherine. She would occasionally emerge with bad news or new corporate procedures, which were also bad news.

Three hundred and twelve e-mails were what he figured between his personal inbox and the one from the website. But fifty-seven of them were in the junk mail folder, some might say. That was only helpful if you didn't have to look at all of them to make sure they weren't customer or vendor correspondence. One, one and two. Beth plus Sandra equals double misery to come. He sighed.

"You have reached the voice mailbox of Patric Zulli,"

he said. "I am unable to take your pho-phone call right now, but if you leave a message, I'll get back to you as soon as I can. Thanks and have a... great day." Good enough, said his finger to the pound key as he replaced the receiver. He had most of it right. Their Customer Care Standard was to re-record the message every day and say the date, noting any times he would be away from his desk in a meeting that day, but Patric was too tired to think about it right now. The coffee was bitter and the news was bad. He had eighteen months of additional servitude added to his sentence, not to mention five point five months of pregnancy hormone moodiness from Sandra to look forward to. He would remember to summon the energy to fix his voice mail by Wednesday. At the latest.

"Fifty-fifty for breast cancer?"

Oh, what fresh hell is this? Patric turned from his computer to face two bright and shiny faces from the Staff Committee. Tia Something and he couldn't remember. Were they suggesting those were the odds of survival or did they think that his two dollars or three for five would make a difference to the cell doubling rate of the metastasis?

He opened his top drawer and fished around in the compartment under his pen tray for a couple dollars in change, keeping his eye open for the perfect worry dolls for these two with their aggressively charitable pink ribbon t-shirts. A single strip of Ruban invisible tape would cover the both of them and their hopeful mouths so he wouldn't have to listen to their shrill voices anymore. Because they went away when he gave them the money, he decided not to bother. Maybe another day.

It was nine-oh-eight by the clock on his computer,

although the clock on his cell phone displayed a more optimistic nine-ten. This all went back to Grade Twelve: tension between Patric and his father, one useless guidance counselor and a decision to pursue a Liberal Arts education. He could be making real money now if he'd followed his father's advice of apprenticing in one of the trades. But because he had suggested it, Patric chose the opposite. The opposite of plumber is historian. The opposite of Bachelor is husband. The opposite of Arts is crafts. Or sciences, business, etc. There wasn't much that was Artistic about this job or his seven co-workers. But for Beth, it would soon be history.

Tuesday

Beth didn't show up for work the next day and neither did Sandra. Great, thought Patric. Now he'd have to pick up the error report e-mails from all the portal users as well as his own work. What else could go wrong? One thing he had done right was get himself a Starbucks extra bold on the way in to work. The stuff was literally tweaking his brain as he logged onto the network. Screw Brew Rite Coffee… this was the level of alertness he needed in this place.

"Patric Zulli?"

He looked up from his keyboard to see a dark-haired man in a neat gray suit standing beside his desk. Where did he come from? "Yes?" said Patric.

"Come with me," said the man.

"Sorry, you are?"

"Mr. Sanchez."

Must be some goon from the corporate side. Maybe they're finally going to follow up on his complaint about Catherine and her bullshit promotion policies. He shrugged.

"Okay," said Patric, picking up his coffee and following Sanchez out of the department to... who knows? They walked down the back corridor, waited wordlessly for the elevator to arrive and then they got on and the doors closed behind them. They started ascending even though there were no buttons pressed. Patric looked at him. "Which floor do you want?"

"I've come about the spells," said Sanchez.

Patric blinked several times while processing this. Finally, he said, "Sorry again, what?"

"The two voodoo proxies and the binding incantations you uttered with intent. The fixing has already begun and I've just come about the cost."

Sanchez stood squarely facing him with his hands clasped in front of him. Patric looked above the elevator doors at the floor indicators, which weren't lighting up although they were still moving. He pressed the button for the seventh floor, home of the megacube, which he was wishing he had never left.

"The two voodoo," said Patric. "What, you mean the little dolls in the paper clips?"

"That you purchased on your first trip to the home of your maternal grandmother."

He took a sip of coffee and cocked his head like a dog. "My Guatemala trip?"

"Yes. Your grandmother was a voodoo practitioner and she passed on this art to her daughter, who passed it on to you.

"Mom? She never cast any spells on anyone," he said.

Sanchez smiled. "The blood bond is unbroken or I wouldn't be here."

"Huh," he said, wondering what dark arts his mother had gotten up to before joining the... wait, what the fuck? There was no such thing as voodoo magic.

"You're probably thinking there's no such thing as magic," said Sanchez. "But there is. And voodoo magic comes at a cost to those who can wield it. This will take the form of physically weakening you each time you perform a rite—unless you can capture some talisman with personal significance to the object of your spell to function as your power source."

"Okay," said Patric. "Never mind. I take them back. I don't want anything bad to happen to Beth or Sandra, as annoying as they may be."

"Something bad is already happening," said Sanchez. "And undoing a spell has its own costs."

The elevator stopped suddenly and the doors opened on the seventh floor. Patric stepped out immediately and Sanchez turned, but didn't follow him out.

"You think about it and let me know," said Sanchez as the doors were closing. "I'll come again tomorrow."

Patric looked at the sealed doors and then up and down the empty corridor. What the hell just happened?

Wednesday

Patric woke up in his small one bedroom apartment with a dump truck parked on his chest. Jesus, how did that pull in here and how did he sleep through it? He rolled over onto his side and coughed, trying to get some air in. He could barely stand up, but he managed to stagger to the kitchen for some toast, which stuck in his throat. He put the rest of it in the garbage. His eyelids were like window blinds and someone was tugging on the cords. All he wanted was to go back to bed, but he had to make it in to work to see what was going on and monitor the Sanchez situation. Was this the cost he mentioned? If so, he couldn't afford it.

He skipped the shower, bought two high speed turbo coffees for himself at Starbucks and shuffled and groaned his way into the office by quarter past nine. He stopped in at the megacube to consult with Catherine before entering the pen. She looked up when he leaned on her door frame, spilling coffee on his hand.

"Ouch," he said.

"Oh," said Catherine. "Good morning, Patric. You don't look well. Should you be here?"

"Yeah, fine," he said, which was a complete lie, vis–à–vis the dump truck he was now carrying on his shoulders, the toast lump which was still traveling down his esophageal tube in slow motion and the old man legs he was arthritically hobbling around on, but what the hell. "How are Beth and Sandra today? I mean, have you heard from them?"

"Yes," she said. She looked at him strangely and then continued. "Beth called in sick again and Sandra was taken to hospital with pregnancy complications and is now in Intensive Care on bed rest."

"So we're two short?" he said. He tried not to gulp audibly.

"Yes, so if you could—"

"Monitor the portal e-mails, sure."

"Okay."

She watched him leave with what could have been described as a suspicious look on her face. Did he look like a petty and vindictive voodoo practitioner who could have caused all this? Come on, Catherine. Get your head in the game! To believe that, you'd have to believe in… magical powers or something.

He fell into his chair, exhausted. This situation was out of control. While he was gulping down some fairly hot coffee, he looked up at the ugly ceramic pig sitting atop a pile of binders on the top shelf of Sandra's cubicle. Day in and day out it sat there beaming at her in cockeyed pink beneficence, thanks to her four-year-old, who had made it for her. It was an object of great personal significance to her, one that made her heart swell up with pride and her eyes water like a windy day on top of a roller coaster.

He took a look around the department to make sure all eyes were on work, and then he grabbed the pig from the top of the wall and set it on the desk in front of him. He searched his mind for a suitable incantation, eyes resting on the worry doll in the paper clip which represented Sandra. Taking the pig in hand, he focused on the little doll and spoke aloud in a whisper: *When this breaks, so breaks my spell; thus will you and your baby be well.* He smashed the pig in the bottom of his garbage can and pulled Sandra off the wall and out of the paper clip, dropping her back into his pen tray, free as a Guatemalan worry bird.

"Sorry," he said to the wondering glances he was getting from the rest of the department. "Broke my mug."

"Doesn't it feel better with that dump truck off your shoulders?"

Patric startled and spun his chair around to find Mr. Sanchez in his immaculate suit, leaning against the cubicle opposite his. His heart jumped out of neutral right into high gear. It smelled like someone had lit a match.

"Where did you come from?" said Patric.

"Same place as yesterday," said Mr. Sanchez. He stood up and began walking towards the exit corridor. "Walk with me, Patric."

What options did he have here? The appearance of Mr. Sanchez wasn't exactly good news, but he was Patric's only source of information at the moment. Oh, luckless lapse in judgment that ever let him buy those stinkin' voodoo miniatures from that market stall in *Villa Nueva*! He got up and followed Sanchez out and through the grid, a hopeless feeling settling in his guts with the coffee. When they were back on the elevator that went up, up, up to nowhere, Sanchez began.

"So," he said. "You learn fast."

"Well, since my own mother doesn't seem to have taught me anything, necessity played mommy to my invention today."

"Good man. So you have settled one account, but that still leaves one other. Unpaid debts don't go away on their own."

"Give me time. I'll figure something out, now that I have some idea what I'm doing. And, okay, don't take this the wrong way, but let's say I try this again in the future—not that I will, but let's just say. If I can figure out the, um, payment, before I say the spell, will that mean I don't ever have to see your smiling face again?"

"Hurtful!" Sanchez grabbed his heart in mock surprise. "What, you don't like talking to me? Haven't I given you good advice?"

"I wouldn't say that you have, no."

"Come on. You would've woken up this morning under that weight with no idea what was going on."

"Okay, I'll give you that. So, is that what you do? Is this your job?"

"Yes," said Sanchez. He adjusted the cuff of his jacket and brushed a speck of something off his lapel. "I'm in charge of maintaining balance in the magical community."

"Wow," said Patric. "You must travel a lot."

"Well, not in the conventional sense, but I do get around."

"But are you a real person, too?"

"Of course, just like you."

"You have a family and all that?"

"Sure. Two kids and a wife."

"Oh. Got any pictures?"

Sanchez nodded proudly and pulled a wallet out of his back pocket. He removed a folding section and passed it over to Patric. He looked closely at two dark-haired, dark-eyed smiling lads wearing sports team shirts. So... ordinary. Patrick shook his head in wonder and folded it back up, passing it to Sanchez. "Nice," he said.

"Thanks," said Sanchez. He replaced that section of his wallet and put it back into his pocket. "So, be efficient with your spells and you won't need to worry about me. But if you start casting without keeping things in balance, I'll be in touch."

Sanchez looked neither threatening nor friendly about this statement. It was just a frank, matter of fact kind of look he was giving him as the elevator came to a stop and the doors opened behind him. Patric didn't like the look one bit.

Thursday

Beth was back at work again and Sandra was out of the hospital and recovering at home. Patric was glad to see Beth. Not happy, but relieved. He had managed to scoop Beth's Korean bride and groom figurines during a quiet moment during lunch and break the spell on her, so everything was back to normal. Normal as in the usual misery—no more, no less.

Friday

When it came time for Beth's goodbye lunch, Patric tried to get a seat beside her. Maybe some of her good vibes might penetrate his cells. He ended up one seat away because Catherine muscled him aside with her bossiness, but Beth's bubbly excitement had no trouble reaching him. She talked so much during lunch that her chicken *quesadilla* went half uneaten. It might also have been that it was a bit heavy on the cilantro as it so often was.

He had taken his turn signing the good-bye card and given his five dollars towards a travel money belt for her. Carefully, he taped the Beth worry doll into the card next to his signature, leaving her head free so she could breathe. *Put this under your pillow,* he wrote in the card, *and all your worries will be absorbed by the doll. Good luck on your adventures. Your co-worker, Patric.*

Maybe a better person would have written *friend.* But his good feelings only stretched so far. Anyway, he was only half concentrating on the conversation around him, preferring to think about Catherine's locket and the picture of Sanchez's sons that he had hidden away in his desk. The first was the key to his soon-to-be career advancement and the second an insurance policy against interference from Mr. Sanchez. This time, he was going to do things right. Magic was a powerful weapon. You just had to use it carefully.

Auto Loss

Holly's manager handed her a yellow file folder. "Here's a house fire we just got in by fax," she said. Alisa was a six-foot tall, no-nonsense Jamaican woman who'd seen it all and could give you a look with her mouth set and chin tilted down and her eyes wide open and unblinking that said, 'Don't even start with me.' And no one did. It was a signature look. "Can you open a new claim and call the insured this afternoon?"

"Yes," said Holly. She was picking up voice mail in one ear, listening to her boss with the other, and nodding at both. Holly was slim and petite with light brown no work short hair. She had a pretty face, her mother told her, but she should smile more.

Alisa nodded back and started to walk away. "Oh, yeah," she said over her shoulder. "One of the insureds is deceased."

"What?" said Holly, hanging up the phone, but her boss was already gone. She looked at the thin yellow file on her desk. Yellow for a property loss. Red for auto, green for go. Blue for Mondays, black for... deceased. She closed her eyes for a three count, and when she opened them it was still there. She looked around at the pile of colored files on her desk, then at the clock on her computer. It was almost 3:00, which meant there wasn't much time left to call. She sighed and opened the cover.

Couch caught fire in basement while husband asleep and he died. Wife can be reached at phone # above, the broker had scrawled on the loss report.

She looked around her desk for something more important to do than call a woman whose house had just burned down, but there was nothing. The image of the couch on fire and the sleeping husband was stuck in the basement of her brain stem. It wasn't a violent image. It was almost peaceful the way he was just sleeping there and she pictured the flames as the warm glow of a fireplace all around him. Sleeping like a log. She tried a smile at this thought but it wouldn't come. She picked up her mug and started across the floor towards the kitchen. The office was pretty quiet, despite the trills of many phones and the low murmurs of cubicle phone conversations. A faint whiff of coffee and perfume lingered in the air, underlying the usual dusty carpet notes that clung to invisible lines in the air like laundry.

Martin from Underwriting was getting a coffee so he poured a cup for her also. She smiled and thanked him. When he left the room, she wandered over to look at the new postings while she waited for her coffee to cool, blowing on it occasionally and taking small sips. Then Alisa came in and looked at her before offering a quizzical How's it going and Holly decided she couldn't delay any longer.

She dialed the number as soon as she got back to her desk.

"Hello?"

"Hello, may I speak with Mrs. Bennett, please?"

"Yes, just a moment."

Holly tapped a pen on the rim of her coffee cup and closed her eyes while she heard the faint background sounds of a woman calling out and some sounds of movement and then a sharp clunk.

"Hello?"

"Hello, Mrs. Bennett?"

"Yes."

"Hi, it's Holly Maynard calling from your insurance company." She took a deep breath. "I was very sorry to hear of your loss."

"Thank-you," said Mrs. Bennett. "I still can't believe it happened."

Holly picked up her pen and pushed the file over to her right. "I know how difficult this must be. Are you okay to talk a little bit about the fire?"

"Yes, I think so. It was one day ago. Two nights."

"Okay. I'd like to send somebody out to see your basement. Would that be all right?"

"I never went back to sleep. I was so angry with him. Then I smelled smoke. Sorry, dear. What were you saying?"

"Can I send someone out to see your basement?"

"Yes. When?"

Holly looked at her watch, but couldn't focus on the time. "His name is Jason and I'll get him to give you a call today. Have you got somewhere to stay?"

"Yes, this is at… I'm at my sister's right now. This is her number."

"Okay, but if it becomes a problem, let me know, and we'll put you up in a hotel. Keep any receipts from eating out and send them to me. Do you have my number?"

"Yes, my broker gave it to me."

"Okay, well, again, my name is Holly. You call me if you have any questions." Then she slipped into the routine. "Let me just explain quickly what's going to happen. Jason will come and see you today. He'll take a statement from you, and look around your basement."

"A statement?"

"Yes, just tell him what happened."

"Oh, okay."

"We'll get a clean-up crew in there, and a restoration contractor for any repairs. Jason will help you make a list of all the things that were burnt or smoke damaged, and we will replace those items for you."

"Mmm hmm." Her voice was barely audible.

"I'll let you go now, Mrs. Bennett. And again, I'm very sorry."

The phone went dead.

Holly wrote in the file, and then turned to the computer to set up the new claim. Then she called Jason, the field claims rep, and left a message on his cell phone. Called the Fire Marshall's office and asked for the report to be faxed over. Made notes on the system regarding her conversation with the insured. Picked up her voice mail, which was already bulging like a steam boiler about to blow. She hummed a tune to herself that she made up as she went along. Couldn't remember any songs.

We will replace all the things that were burnt. *So stupid.* Why did she say that?

The drive over to her mother's. Picking up the kids. The drive home. Requests for hot dogs for dinner. Hamburger Helper instead. Walking the dog in the park. Kids playing and then home to bed. Doing the dishes. Quiet.

As she got into bed she noticed the room was already cold, which was odd, so she got back up to check the thermostat. It was supposed to turn itself up and down automatically, an electronic one. The last thing she needed was for the furnace to go out on her. She turned on the hall light and peered at the little readout window. One of the kids must have been playing with it and pressed the down arrow so that it went to the low setting at 7:00pm instead of 10:00pm. She adjusted the time and closed the flap.

It was one of those nights she couldn't seem to be tired. At first she lay there and tried her breathing exercises to calm her mind, imagining each part of her body relaxing one by one. And then she switched to her Positive Thinking podcasts on her iPod, the soothing voice in her head repeating all those reasonable-sounding platitudes. She tried reading her book. Then she just gave up and stared at the ceiling. Let her mind wander where it wanted to go: to thoughts of the widow Bennett and what she lost in the fire.

* * *

Holly's desk had the look of a busy person, she thought to herself over her coffee the next morning. There were files piled everywhere and sticky notes and lists of phone numbers up on the cubicle walls, on the sides of her computer monitor, on the desktop and all over. None of these collections of ceramic dogs or

Kinder Egg surprise toys you sometimes see, none of this kids' artwork with bright splatters of paint or crayon stick figures, no pictures of kids.

Jason walked toward her from the cubicle row alongside the windows and put his briefcase down on her desk. She looked first at his briefcase on her desk and then up at him. He smiled.

"So, do you want to hear what happened with that Bennett guy?" he said.

She nodded. "Sure." Drained the last gulp of her coffee, put the mug down, reached for a pen just to have something in her hands and sat back in her chair. Jason was stocky but not quite fat with dark curly hair and a thick unibrow. He had the Van Dyke goatee that all the guys were sporting and was wearing the trench coat that he thought made him look like a private investigator. His fingernails were always clean and trimmed.

"Drunk as a fuckin' skunk." He waited for her reaction with raised eyebrows and then pressed on. "You'd have to be pretty looped to catch on fire and not notice, right?"

"The smoke gets them before the fire does," she said. The orange light of the first catch of flames had barely illuminated the couch as the smoke filled the dark room. She felt that she should be taking notes or something, so she reached for the file.

He looked at her for a second, then nodded and took a piece of paper out of his case and put it on her desk. "Official cause of death was smoke inhalation, according to the M.E.'s report. The cop gave me that. So the old lady didn't have anything to do with it. I guess the old guy got kicked out of bed 'cause he was so liquored up or whatever, and he got cold in the basement and pulled the couch up to the woodstove to keep warm. A real brainiac, huh?"

She nodded and looked down to make a note. He looked disappointed that she wasn't getting his sense of humor.

"Mrs. Bennett smelled smoke and called 911, so the house was saved." He pulled a sheet of paper out of his briefcase. "Here's my site inspection. Most of the finished basement is toast, and there's smoke and water damage everywhere, so kiss all the upholstery goodbye and the carpets. Most of the rest of it can be cleaned. I've got my guy in there right now trying to decide if there is any structural damage."

"Did you cut her a check, yet?" said Holly.

"Nope," he said, zipping up his briefcase. "Hey, you want to get a coffee with me?"

She looked at him, at his hesitant smile and then realized he meant here in the office. She nodded and smiled, grabbing her mug and following him down the hall towards the kitchen. Jason poured himself a cup and then one for her. They chatted about her pending file count and his. How it had been so long since there was a long weekend. Jason seemed to be listening to her very intently with a good amount of eye contact. Not too much. He was leaning against the counter, his head tilted a bit to the side.

"So, listen," he said after a while. "I was wondering if you'd like to get some dinner some time."

She looked at him and it was almost like she couldn't register his words. She felt the strange intimacy of his posture and the smile on his face and in his eyes, but the verbal cues weren't reaching her.

"Or a movie?" he continued.

Then it clicked. "Oh... sorry, no. It's just that, with

55

the kids… it's too hard to get a sitter."

He nodded and kept smiling. "I know what you mean. What if I could find you a sitter? I have a couple of nieces who look after my kids if I have to go out when it's one of my nights to have them at my place."

She smiled back at him with steady finality in her eyes, holding his gaze. "I don't think so. Thanks, anyway, Jason." She started walking back towards her desk with her full coffee mug, careful not to spill it. Sat down and got to work on her voice mail. She could've been flattered that he'd asked and that this clearly reaffirmed that she was an attractive, interesting sort of person. She could've been intrigued by his offer and imagined seeing a whole new side of Jason. She could've been offended, as office romances weren't exactly encouraged. She could've been annoyed at his timing, or secretly pleased but not with him in a thousand years, or uncertain, or felt any one of a hundred other things, but the bottom line was she just didn't date.

Typing away, updating the Bennett file, the phone ringing, and then the surprise of Mrs. Bennett on the line just as she'd been thinking about her.

"Yes, this is Holly."

Why did this file have to come to me? What do I say to this woman? She smoothed her eyelids down with her thumb and fingertip as if the pain of her headache might be coming in through her eyes.

"Jason was at the house," said Mrs. Bennett, a quavering voice on the line.

"Yes. He told me. Is there anything you need?"

"No, I just wanted to know what was going to happen next."

Holly adjusted the phone and opened her eyes to

look at the file in front of her. "Well, first we have to get your house back to habitable condition, and then we can get you some money to start replacing your belongings. We'll have to see what the contractor finds."

"I see."

There was a long pause. Holly cleared her throat. "Mrs. Bennett?"

"Yes?"

"Is there anything I can do for you?"

"It's all so confusing."

Holly waited, twisting the phone cord around her finger.

"There's been the life insurance guy, the funeral home, there's you people, there's the rest of the finances, and Harold always dealt with that stuff. And then there's just… what do I do now?"

She shook her head to nobody. "I don't know."

Mrs. Bennett sighed on the line. "I'm sorry, dear. I'll let you go. I'm sure you're busy."

"Do you have any children?" said Holly.

"A daughter. She lives in Alberta. She's flying in tomorrow."

"Well, that's good." She unwound the phone cord from her finger. "Give me a call if there's anything you need. We'll get things… we'll get your house back in order as soon as we can."

"Thank-you, Holly."

"Good-bye."

She hung up the phone and looked around her desk at the many things she could be doing right now, her almost cold coffee, voice mail light blinking, pile after pile of folders.

* * *

It wasn't until the drive home that Holly thought about Mrs. Bennett again, and then what she thought was, it's almost over. Jason will handle most of it from here, and I probably won't have to talk to her again. This made her feel lighter somehow, and she even sang a song with the boys in the car on the way home like they used to.

After dinner, they were eager to get out for their walk, so they all put on their stuff. This took about a half hour of arguing over what to wear: not sneakers, it has to be boots; you have to wear snow pants if you want to go off the path; no, you can't wear a bicycle helmet instead of a hat. The dog had to sit watching all this, holding his leash in his mouth and wagging patiently. Chester, her third child; the one who came first. The nurturing practice run. As it was quite cold, they even put the sweater tube on him, which he tolerated.

Ryan and David ran along the path ahead with sticks they had found and pretended to be power robots or something, their light-heartedness a thing of beauty. She wanted to be right there with them, just entirely in the moment the way kids are. Their frosty breath came out in plumes before them. The dog bounced along beside her and sniffed out various tufts and tree roots. The boys were playing close to the riverbank and Holly was about to tell them to stick to the path when David started yelling.

"Mommy!" he yelled, jumping up and down. "I think I see'd a fish looking out at me."

"Keep back from the edge," she said. "You can see him from the path. You know the rules."

"Mom, where do the fish go in winter?" asked Ryan. He tapped his stick against the sidewalk and looked up at her as if she had all the answers in the world.

"I don't think they go anywhere," she said, looking out at the thin ribbon of snow-covered ice and imagined the darkly flowing river beneath. "I think they just stay under the ice and keep very still in the dark near the bottom. When spring comes they start moving around again and look for food." She thought of what it must be like for the fish, something still warm at the core, but trapped in an ice prison for months on end.

"Huh," said Ryan.

Just then they noticed a man coming toward them, walking a dog, so Ryan and David ran over to meet him and pet his dog. Holly followed after them, keeping a tight hold on Chester's leash just in case.

"That's a really nice dog, mister," said Ryan, kneeling down with his brother and petting the excited animal, having to fend off many licks to the face. "What kind is he?"

"He's a border collie," said the man. "Full of energy, as always." He looked up at Holly as she approached. "You can pet him—he won't bite. Is this your Mommy?"

"Yes," said David, looking up at her. "Our Daddy died."

"Shut up, stupid," said Ryan, looking over at her quickly, old enough to know the things they didn't talk about. Holly looked down at the little dog, a stuck smile on her face.

"I'm sorry," said the man, looking at her. "Was

this… recent?"

"June," she said without looking up at him. "It happened in June."

* * *

On her way to the bathroom the next morning, she saw Jason coming the other way and tried to catch his eye to smile at him and nod, do the professional thing, but he just looked down and pulled out his cell phone as if he didn't see her. He was looking very rumpled in his trench coat. Was it always going to be awkward between them now? She continued on to the ladies room without looking back.

Holly sat in the third stall from the doorway. Why had he asked her out on a date, anyway? Did she all of a sudden look ready to date? It wasn't that long ago that she would leave the office to cry in this very stall, when she first got back to work after… was it really eight months ago? Aren't you a widow for one year, officially? He should respect that. Did he even know about Andrew? How long had she worked with Jason, anyway? She looked at her bare ring finger and remembered taking her ring off after the funeral and putting it on the dresser. And never having the urge to put it on since. Why did she have to think about this? How had this giant, puffy sadness she had spent all her time keeping pushed down and tucked away gone on this long? The lack of crying still felt new.

At first, the tears had scared her. They came in waves of sobbing she couldn't control, like something washing over her. The kids were scared of her, the dog would whimper, and her mom would grab the whole lot and take them out for a walk. Andrew was her high school yearbook co-editor, best friend and confidante. They went to the same college for journalism and got married two months after graduation. She wasn't a widow; she was an amputee.

After her bereavement leave and vacation time had run out last July, she'd had to pull it together. But it's not like there was a smooth transition for her. After a week of crying jags at the office and a sick day long weekend contemplating how she could keep on going to work like this, she got in the elevator the second Monday back and it was like she flicked a switch and there was no feeling. She pulled herself together and that was that. It hurt every time she looked at Andrew's freckles and beautiful red hair on the two children he left behind, but it was an academic thing, as if she were the chief lab technician registering her feelings and responses from behind a glass partition. Almost a year now. First Christmas without him, first Valentine's Day, David's Birthday... her emotions were removed from her, at a safe distance. Behind airtight, pressurized, tempered, shatter-proof glass.

A car crash. It's a blessing that he was alone when it happened, the family told her. A terrible thing all the same. The kind of banal claim details that happened all the time here. The indifference of the independent adjusters assigned to handle the file, not recognizing the name. The car written off, the death benefit paid, the Family Law Act claims honored. Just another auto loss. It was actually cheaper when they died: $25,000 puts them in the ground, as opposed to the millions of dollars it cost for the veggies and quads that hung on. All the gallows humor of the insurance industry a background noise she heard every day: If you run over a pedestrian and see him in your rear-view mirror still moving around, back up and finish him off.

It felt like her kids were on the other side of that glass, too. She couldn't connect with them the same way she used to. She only had so much patience for playtime and goofing around and then she needed a break from them altogether. Sometimes this felt like she was a bad mother. But at least she was there for them, still holding it together despite everything, and she was able to cut herself some slack for this reason. It's the way it is for now, not forever. The calm and sensible voice of her grief counselor from months ago.

The boys knew about the glass, too. Could feel the difference in her—especially Ryan, her big boy. The way he looked at her sometimes, as though he wanted to ask her a question but was staying quiet and being patient. There was a bit of Andrew in that look. A bit of Andrew in a lot of things she saw in him these days, stuck inside him the way the burning husband had gotten stuck in her, the flames always there with him, but the temperature remaining the same. It was mostly just smoke. Would Mrs. Bennett wake up smelling that smoke every day forever? Certain things stay with us.

She put herself together, washed her hands, looked at her face in the mirror. No signs of cracks forming. She fixed her hair (startled to remember she still had a hairstyle and still made it to the salon every couple of months), smoothed down her skirt and went back to work.

* * *

Holly went looking for Jason and found him in the kitchen finishing his lunch.

"Hi, Holly," he said and looked away. "I was just, um…"

"Hi, Jason," said Holly. She stood there resolutely. When she caught his eye, she began. "I just wanted you to understand that I've got two kids, a dog, a house, a dead husband and a car that's making a funny noise, just so you're aware. But if you're okay with all that, yes, I'd like to go out with you. If your offer still stands."

"Yes, it does," he said. "Holly, I already knew all that when I asked you. Well, except for the funny noise. I just want you to understand that I know nothing about car engines."

She laughed. "That's okay."

"So, do you have a babysitter?"

"Yes, my mother. We won't have to take the kids with us."

"Good start. Would Saturday night work, then?"

"That's what I was thinking. Weeknights are too much of a rush."

"Good. Yes. How about I pick you up at around 7:00?"

"Sure. You'll need, um, why don't I just e-mail you my address and cell phone number?"

"Great."

"Great. And thanks for asking."

"Okay," said Jason. "Have a good lunch." And away he went, back to his desk.

She was left wondering how this all happened. Jason wasn't her perfect man, it couldn't be denied. But she had to start somewhere. It was time. And besides, he had a certain something. Maybe he would grow on her. No, this was good. She was going on a date.

The Badger Hound is Eating my Little Donkey

How did he even reach up to the kitchen table to get it, with his stumpy legs and sausage body? But there it is on the floor, beans and rice spilling out into a corona of salsa across the kitchen tiles, the wax paper wrapper still clinging to the edge of the chair and a piece of the tortilla slowly disappearing into his mouth like a flat, white tongue. His eyes were on me with what passed for a repentant look, or maybe it was simple guilty pleasure. I only left the room for a few seconds to look for a tissue or a washcloth after spilling some coffee on myself and now this damn calamity.

Jesus, you try to do somebody a favor.

Earlier today, watching Catherine across the table at the faculty meeting, I consciously kept my eyes on her face and away from the pleasing fullness of her sweater. An elegant woman of average height, she had a pretty face and long, serious hair in a ponytail, conservative slacks concealing exciting curves. We'd known each other for a few years, but her situation had recently changed when she broke it off with her former boyfriend. All week I'd been mentally preparing myself to ask her out when, by some miracle, she came up to me after the meeting and gave me a coy smile.

"Brian, are you busy at lunch today?"

This kind of thing happens when one is made a Full Professor of Linguistics, I guessed. Everyone in the department looks at you differently. I smiled and smoothed my hand across my hair on the left side, which sometimes sticks up. "Why, no. I'm not, actually."

"Oh, that's great," she said and rested a hand on my arm. "Can you do me a huge favor?"

"Sure," I said, smile fading, but still looking hopefully into her eyes. Could this be a version of *Do me the honor of having lunch with me?* Do me this favor? Going out with someone could be considered doing them a favor. Maybe not a huge one.

"Can you let my dog out of my apartment for a quick walk? I always check on him at midday, but I have a lunch date today."

I blinked at her, scanning her face as this sank in. *She's going out with someone else and I'm looking after her dog?* "Of course, Catherine. Think nothing of it."

I patted her hand to let her know she could count on me, taking her key. I watched her make her way to the door, stopping for occasional small talk as people were filing out on their way back to their offices or lecture halls or off to insipid, ill-advised romantic encounters during terribly overpriced lunches. Probably with Dr. Jacobson, that complete ass from Social Sciences.

And later, when I was sitting in the Drive-Thru lane at Taco Town, it came to me. She must think I'm a nice guy. I've somehow been pigeon-holed into the role of the reliable colleague... a man with whom she is and always will be "just friends." And now here I am, doing

her this huge favor. I'm standing here in this beautiful
modern kitchen. Her key is resting safely in my pocket.
The coffee spill is drying on my houndstooth jacket.
The dachshund is eating my burrito.

Awkward Stages

Frank's Wager

(Blowing) Check, check. *(Tapping noise)* It's working.

Frank Powers: Good. Okay. Can I get you a coffee or something? I can't guarantee I'll get the, uh, machine working, but I'll give it a shot. Usually I just walk over to Timmies.

Interviewer: No, thanks. I'm fine.

Frank Powers: So what publication has sent you here today?

Interviewer: Quill and Quire.

Frank Powers: Oh, excellent.

Interviewer: Yes. I'll just, um, say what we're doing. This is an interview with Frank Powers. We're meeting on October 15th, 2007. My name is James Cholkan.

Frank Powers: Nice to meet you, James.

Interviewer: Nice meeting you. I'm a huge fan. So, many of your fans complain that you haven't produced a novel in over six years. What have you been working on lately?

Frank Powers: Mostly reminiscences. I'm sure most of it would be incoherent without my editor to patch it all together. He snips away the stray threads.

Interviewer: So it's autobiographical?

Frank Powers: No, not the way I write it.

Interviewer: Oh... You have been described as one of the greatest post-modern existentialists. How has this philosophy informed your life experience?

Frank Powers: Well, I was never a philosopher. Post-modern, maybe. But I was always more of a story guy. That other stuff... it's nice to think about, to talk about, but it isn't real. I'm going to get a coffee. Do you want one?

(Rustling noises)

Interviewer: Sure.

Frank Powers: If I can get out of this chair, that is. (Rustling noise followed by crash) Don't worry about it. The cleaning lady comes this Friday.

Interviewer: Really, the coffee isn't necessary.

Frank Powers: All I've got is the awful store brand. Where are the damn filters? Maybe the drawer... no, shit... oh, the closet. Here we are. I'm getting senile. I never know how many scoops to put in. Now, I push this back in and Click, the light goes on and, shit! Clear. Wait, there's the brown. How does that work? I need a new coffee maker.

Interviewer: So we were discussing your thoughts on existentialism.

Frank Powers: So we were. And here I am obsessing about my coffee and ignoring such an important topic. Although coffee is an important topic all by itself. It's personal, it's social. It's a necessary start to the day or mid-morning perk up or the completion of a good meal. It's like... it's like the history of us together was mapped out by the coffee we drank. What magical property does it hold? How many couples have come together over coffee? Even when we met, the first thing we did was go for coffee—maybe there's a story in that —and then to lunch, dinner, and then the rest of our lives. And what a wonderful life we had. Here, it's ready now.

(Clinking of mugs, followed by pouring)

Interviewer: Thanks.

Frank Powers: I don't have any cream, but there's probably some sugar around here. *(Slurping noise)*

Interviewer: No, this is fine. How did you—

Frank Powers: Well, it's all right, but it's not great. I haven't made a decent cup of coffee in six years. Has it really been six years? I can't stop thinking about her. The way my study is furnished, the decorating, the flowered wallpaper we put up together in the bathroom, the way the coffee maker won't work… everything makes me want to be with her again. Only sixty-eight, so young.

Interviewer: I'm sorry. How did she die?

Frank Powers: Heart attack. Died of a broken heart, literally, and broke mine in the process. Unbearable irony. I can't even write stories with "Affairs of the Heart" in them. The heart isn't what brings people together; it's the organ which fractures. That little piece of muscle and tubes, responsible for so much, and when it breaks down…

Interviewer: It must be hard to lose someone you clearly loved so much. *(A long pause)* Mr. Powers? Do you want to take a break or keep going?

Frank Powers: Call me Frank. No, let's keep going.

Interviewer: Okay, Frank. I'll try to get through these remaining questions, if that's okay. I don't want to take up too much of your time. Well, then, how do you place yourself in the body of post-modern work of this century?

Frank Powers: Oh, Financially well-off. Lucky. I made a living doing what I love and that is a tremendous blessing not to be underestimated. Do you know how many writers are out there scraping by driving cabs or collecting garbage or teaching at universities?

Interviewer: I mean in terms of post-war thematic evolution.

Frank Powers: I don't know. I never really understood all that terminology and classification. I just write stories.

Interviewer: I see where you're going. Sort of a "Fiction of the Blasé," post-Freudian, de-classificationalism?

Frank Powers: I guess so.

Interviewer: Okay. Hemingway once said that his later years were brimming with confidence and optimism.

Frank Powers: (*Laughs*) And then he blew his brains out.

Interviewer: Well, yes, but that came later. Do you consider your latest work to be full of this same confidence now that you are reaching the "pinnacle" of your craft?

Frank Powers: No, not really. I am prone to self-doubt. I can't even make a decent cup of coffee. All that stuff that you call existentialism... that was a long time ago; I was a different person then. I don't know what I believe in now, but I know what I know: I'm lonely and I miss my wife. I've started thinking about the concept of a spiritual afterlife and whether I'll see her again when I die.

Interviewer: You mean the quote unquote afterlife?

That would be an about face from your earlier, anti-religious work. Are you saying you've come to believe in God? *(Laughs)*

Frank Powers: There are people who believe in God and people who don't and I think it's okay to be either. And I don't think you can convince yourself to be either one, you just are. What happened to me was probably what happens to a lot of guys who've been married for 42 years and then lose their wives to a broken down heart. Or breast cancer. That's a nasty one. So you roll around in an empty house, not sure what to do or how to occupy yourself or what's important to you now you're on your own and just constantly talking to yourself. Well, I went on talking to myself like that for months until I realized that I wasn't talking to myself, I was talking to God. And I guess I'd been angry with him for a long time without knowing it. So, anyway, we made our peace and now we're cool.

Interviewer: You and God are cool? Seriously? The author of No Sense of Direction has found religion?

Frank Powers: I know it sounds funny. Look, it's like this. The biggest presence in my life right now is an absence. I miss her all the time, every day. So I made a deal with God that I would believe in him if I could see her again in the afterlife, whatever you want to call that and whatever it looks like. Heaven, maybe. Have you heard of Pascal's wager?

Interviewer: The unbelievably cynical viewpoint that you might as well keep your options open, just in case belief is a ticket to paradise?

Frank Powers: Exactly the one. Well, I took that bet.

Interviewer: But believing in heaven means believing in the bible, which, as you yourself have taken great pains to point out, is a deeply flawed document.

Frank Powers: I know. I still think that. But I took the bet because I don't care if the afterlife is the same as the heaven in the bible or different, just as long as it's somewhere. Believe me, it still feels weird to think this way. You want some more coffee?

Interviewer: No. So let me get this straight. You made a deal with God, the guy who supposedly wrote a book about agrarian dispute resolution in the pre-Bronze Age Middle East; the guy who takes voice mail from millions of people every day and never gets back to them... the guy who hasn't updated his blog in, like, 2000 years? That God?

Frank Powers: I think so. Tall guy, flowing white beard?

Interviewer: Do you realize you're substantially recanting the central theme of about half your novels?

Frank Powers: Well, only if you think that was the central theme.

Interviewer: This is unbelievable. What do you think this will do to your fans?

Frank Powers: What I think or don't think now doesn't change any of my earlier novels. They're still exactly the same.

Archival & Special Collections - Resources - University of Guelph Library
Transcript of Podcast Interview
Published as "Introspect/Retrospect - Last Interview with Frank Powers"
Quill & Quire, Vol. 37, No.11
Recorded October 15, 2007
Published posthumously, November 25, 2007

Coming soon from Mark Victor Young
Author of *Awkward Stages*

Lost Paris - *A book of linked short stories* - James Joyce and his wife Nora have an unexpected visit from his newly-engaged brother Stanislaus, but there's no money to be had anywhere! Later, Joyce and Ezra Pound attend a historic concert, but then have a falling out over creative differences. Ernest Hemingway returns to the Paris scene in time to help Pound's wife Dorothy Shakespear get to the hospital to have her baby, but Ezra wants nothing to do with it. Then Hemingway has his own issues with former mentor Gertrude Stein. There's never a dull moment for the American ex-pat crowd in Paris in the year 1926.

Sample Story - *Ezra and Ernest: Paris 1926*

25th September 1926 – Gare de Lyon, Paris

Ezra Pound lounged in a chair at a café table outside Le Train Bleu, watching his friend approach from the main stairs of the station. Hemingway looked tired, poor devil. He sat down in the chair opposite him.

"Well?" said Hem.

"Wot ya recon, sir?" said Ezra.

"I don't know."

"Thanks for coming for my grand send-off."

"You feeling better?"

"Still entirely wore aht. The medicos gave me all the possible taps, tests, analyses, etc. I suppose at this point, I'm just suffering from health." He sighed. "I'll be glad to get back to Rapallo, that's all I know."

"Without Dorothy?"

"I dunno. We've arrived at some kind of impasse."

"And Omar?" said Hem. "What about him? It's doing my head in right now, being separated from Bumby. You don't know what it's like. We're talking about your own flesh and blood, here."

"You know my feelings on them thar bambinos, now. They're not conducive to the woild of letters."

"That's a damn cold way to look at it, Ezra. I got lots of writing done when Bumby was a newborn. You adapt. Your whole life changes... for the better."

Ezra smiled. "I remember your tone wasn't so sanguhween at the news of Hadley being pregnant."

"Maybe," he said. "But you need to give yourself time to fall in love with your own child. That's not going to happen if you're a thousand miles away."

"Are you going to have a coffee?"

"What time is your train?"

Ezra looked across at the big clock above the main platform. "Twenty minutes." He drained the remains of his own cup, which had been cold for almost an hour.

"I won't, then."

They stood up and Ezra began picking up his cases. Ernest helped him with his trunk, lugging it across the crowded lobby of the train station, scene of all Ezra's leave-takings from this, his one-time home.

"Oh, I just heard from Mr. Anthill that he's up and about," said Ezra. "Nasty bout with pneumonia, it turns out."

"Good for George," said Hem. "Figured he was young enough to kick it. I heard his concert got a little crazy... sorry I missed it."

"What about you, Hem? When are you going to get out of this damn purgatory and get on with your life?"

"I wish. Hadley's hundred days just started and I don't know how I'm going to make it."

"Them females sure know how to build us our own poihsonalized Hades, don't they? Fer Khrrisst's sake, why don't you just break free and go be with Pauline over yonder in Piggott, Arkansas?"

"Can't. Hadley won't give me my divorce without this separation from Pauline for the hundred days and Pauline can't have her Catholic wedding without the divorce. If I don't kill myself first."

There was no humor in this remark. Hem looked like a man who had just taken a bullet for a friend and now he was looking for a leather belt to bite down on while they took it out with some whiskey and a dagger.

"Hang in there, Hem, old boy," said Ezra, patting him on the shoulder. "This, too, shall bloody well pass."

"Yes, but so, so slowly."

"Yes."

Ezra put down his bags to wait. He knew that Hem's numero uno reason for staying away, truth be told, was more mercenary, related to staying abroad until the end of the year to avoid paying income tax, some scheme Congress had passed for artists, but he saw no reason to mention this and make the man uncomfortable.

They looked off down the tracks at the train rolling towards where they stood on the platform. The same train on which Hadley had left the suitcase with all Hem's early manuscripts, including his first novel, now lost forever to some railway thief while Hadley was off getting a lemonade or a newspaper or sumfink. Probably best not to mention that little episode, either.

"Ezra," said Hem without looking at him. "After things settle down and you and Dorothy get back together, I want you to consider having Omar come to live with you both. You're a father, now, and that little boy will need you. Don't let him grow up without knowing you."

Ezra looked at his friend, who had tears in his eyes. He reached out and shook his hand, patting his shoulder at the same time.

"You're a good man, Hem," he said. "As for me, I've been stuck living with one woman pregnant and the other one furious for a year and a half. Haven't been able to hear myself cogitate in the slightest. The last baby is out and on its way to a nurse's cottage and there's an end to it. I'm going home to be by myself for a while. Maybe get to work on that journal I've been meaning to get started."

Hem nodded. "Good-bye, my friend. I wish you the best of damn luck."

"You, too," said Ezra. "You and Pauline should come and visit me in Rapallo once all this is over. Being by the sea is good for the soul."

"We might just do that. You still owe me a game of tennis."

The train doors opened and Ezra gave his bags to the porter, shook hands with his friend one last time, said his good-byes and best regards to and climbed up the steps to find his seat. He was on his way back to his normal life at last.

* * *

Dear E.P.'s Parents,

Just a quick note to let you know the baby has arrived and everybody is well. We name him Omar to keep up the poetic tradition. It seems to suit him admirably also. He appears small, neat, very philosophic, and at present the eyes, dark blue, are also in the picture. He has a comical crop of dark brown hair, increasing. I hope you won't be too shocked to hear he is not to return with us to Rapallo just at present. He has already been deposited, in a nice cradle (chosen by my mama) in a little-house-with-garden just outside Paris. Madame Collignon has two children of her own and knows all about bottles and milk and such like... I am anxious to get back now to Rapallo and the terrazza.

Affectionately yours,
Dorothy

* * *

Ten Days Earlier - 15th September 1926 —
Montparnasse, Paris

Hemingway walked along Boulevard du
Montparnasse with the slip of paper in his hands,
looking down each side street and alley as he passed.
He had crossed over the Rue du Cherche-Midi and
was almost as far as the Rue de Sèvres when he found
the alley he was looking for, the one where the studio
of the sculptor Brancusi was located. It was a modest-
looking, mostly non-descript shed with lots of skylights
and probably a very low rent. Might have been an
abandoned workshop or smithy which changed gears
when the artists began invading the Quarter.

He knocked on the door, waited a minute, and then
knocked again. He placed his ear against the door and
held his breath and finally heard a shuffling sound
coming from within. The door opened and there stood
Pound, his thick, tawny hair in disarray and his neck
scarf hanging limply, upside-down, over a dingy-
looking white shirt with the collar askew. He looked
grubby, his eyes bleary from sleep.

"Mr. Hemingway," he said. "You keep tracking me
down. How did you find me this time?"

"Well, Mr. Pound," said Hem. "You've spent so
much of your time looking after others; you shouldn't
be surprised when we want to return the favour. I
heard it from Sylvia, who heard it from Man Ray when
he came into Shakespeare & Company and told her
about the drink he'd had with Brancusi, who was
complaining about his melancholy house guest."

He sighed. "Of course. Well, c'mon in."

Pound shuffled back across the studio to a couch
carved out of half a tree, covered by a cushion and

draped in a dirty sheet. He lay down on it with one long exhalation of breath. Hem closed the door behind him, picked up a chair and put it down next to the head of the couch and sat down facing Ezra.

He looked around the room at the many sculptures, some of which looked complete, maybe, and others which looked to be still in progress. Some could've been pillars made of repeating shapes stretching almost to the ceiling. Strange, handmade-looking furniture was all over the room. There was a giant stone slab table in front of a primitive fireplace and a fine film of plaster dust covered everything. A workbench which ran the length of one wall was full of every kind of sculptor's tools. He blinked and turned his attention to his friend.

"How are you, Ezra? Are you getting out at all?"

Ezra sighed again and rubbed his forehead with the back of his hand. "I'm just so damn tired, Hem."

"Are you writing?"

"No. Things are feeling very... um, pointless right now." His voice quit for a moment and he appeared to be suppressing a sob. "We lost it all, Hem. Some of the best of our generation just... gone forever. And for what? An old bitch gone in the teeth. A botched civilization."

"Yes, well, I'm sure we've all felt that way. But you don't need to solve the world's problems, Ezra. You're a father, now. You just need to pull yourself together for your son."

"I can't do it." He shook his head.

"Sure you can. Let's go get some good strong coffee and a croissant at the Dome. We'll take a walk around the Jardin du Luxembourg, clear your head."

"Hem," he said. "I haven't been off this couch since

you and I went to Neuilly a few days ago. I'm just sleeping or not sleeping or having black ideas all the time. I don't think coffee is gonna cut it." He laughed a short laugh. "Nope."

"Now don't crack up on me, Ezra. I'm not having the best time of it myself right now. I'm not sleeping at all. Separated from the woman I love, my own kid, my home. Staying in Gerald Murphy's studio by myself. Got this horrific case of piles you wouldn't believe... even had to cancel my bicycle trip to Marseilles. Sometimes suicide seems like my only option."

Ezra looked at him for a beat and then smiled. "That's real helpful, Hem. Thanks for all the cheerin' up, ya hear?"

Hem broke into a smile and then laughed at himself. "But you have to stay strong, that's what I'm trying to say. You have people depending on you. So do I."

Ezra nodded, staring off at the fireplace.

"Maybe it's time to get a little help. See what the doctors have to say."

"You mean the fifth floor?" Ezra looked at him.

"Is that where they had you the last time? I mean, it seemed to help. At least it will give you a rest and let them check you out."

"You might be right."

"A nice hospital bed would have to be better than that hollow log you've been sleeping in."

"It's not bad, actually." Ezra laughed. "But the food would have to be better. Brancusi's been feeding me all his favourite traditional Romanian dishes: cabbage rolls, carp in brine, sour soup..."

Hem shuddered. "No wonder you're looking so thin. Where is he, by the way?"

"He went out for some wine and cigarettes. He's in

the middle of a crisis right now. He sold a piece called 'Bird in Space' to a wealthy USA-murrikn, but they stopped it at customs and charged it duty as an 'Industrial Item' instead of giving it an exemption as a work of art. He's all up in arms, poor devil, 'bout them Philistines back in our homeland."

"Good ole' U.S. of A.," said Hem. "If it ain't Puritanism or Capitalism, it doesn't exist."

"Ain't it the gawd damned truth?"

"So, what do you say? Should we find ourselves a taxi and go get you a professional opinion?"

Ezra sighed like it would take all his energy just to stand upright again. He looked down at his feet as if they might not work anymore. "I guess we should."

"Okay, then," said Hem. "Where are your shoes?"

"Never mind my shoes... where's my velvet jacket?"

* * *

Dear Dad,

Next generation (male) arrived.
Both D & it appear to be doing well.
Ford going to U.S. to lecture in October.
Have told him you wd. probably be glad to put him up.

more anon,

                              yrs
                              E.

* * *

Four days before that - 11th September 1926 – Hotel Foyot, Paris

Ezra was back in their room at the Hotel after being away for a few days and he was taking advantage of the time by catching up on his correspondence and gathering some of his books for the coming move over to Brancusi's place. He jotted a quick note to his parents to catch them up on the latest developments over where he was on furrin soil. He couldn't think of the last time he'd written to them, neglecting those filial duties probably all summer long. Had he told them about his l'il opry back in June? He had, he was sure. Where had the summer gone? He felt like he hadn't accomplished anything. Bloody Paris. This is why he'd had to leave in the first place – too many distractions. Too many people who wanted to talk about art rather than getting down to the brass tacks and nitty gritty of actually making the stuff.

There was a knock at the door. What the deuce? Just another interruption if he answered it. He picked up a book and resolved to ignore it. Nobody knew he was here and Dorothy was still at the hospital, so whoever it was could just go pound salt.

"Ezra? Are you in there?"

Khrrisst. It was Hem. The doorknob rattled and he knocked again. Wot ells could go wrong today?

"C'mon, pal. Open up. I bring news from Neuilly. The next generation has arrived!"

Ezra sighed. "Just a second." He got up and opened the door.

"Ezra, my friend," said Hem. "Let me be the first to shake your hand and say congratulations! It's a boy. I was there at the hospital with Dorothy till late last night. She came through it like a champ. I've just been back to the studio to try to catch a few winks and then I came over here to find you. You've got to come see him."

Ezra let go of his friend's strong congratulatory grip and sat back down at the desk by the window. "I'm a little busy here, actually."

Hem kept smiling and sat down across the room in a wingback chair. "What do you mean?"

"I don't think they need any help from me over there and I have things I can be doing around here."

"You don't want to see him?"

"Not especially. Seen one, seen the bunch."

"But this is your son."

"Yes, well..." Ezra straightened up a pile of papers and replaced a pen in the pen holder. He crossed his right leg over his left knee and looked out the window at someone passing on the sidewalk that he didn't recognize. Out of the corner of his eye, he saw Hem shake his head.

"Well," said Hem. "You have to at least register the birth at the Town Hall in Neuilly. It's not far from the hospital."

"It's funny she chose that hospital, don't you think? After I had my guts cut open there by those ignorant damn veterinaries."

"It's the American Hospital, Ezra. She probably did it for you."

"Huh," he said.

"C'mon. Let's go. You have to do this."

Ezra picked up a book and inspected a small tear in

the binding. He put it in the pile with his papers and glanced back across the room. "So, this is what must be done? This duty is the sole purview of the pater familias?"

"It's one of them, sure."

Picking up another stack of letters and other papers, he tried to tap down the loose edges so they would all be lined up. He lay them down next to his pile of books and lined up a row of pencils, brushing some specks of grit onto the floor. He sucked his teeth and tapped his finger on the desk, counting out the beats. He sighed. "Okay. Let's go."

"Excellent," said Hem. He stood up again. "Don't forget your identification papers."

"Yes," said Ezra. He put a few slips of paper in his pocket and put on his velvet jacket. They walked out together, passing through the lobby and out to the sidewalk. He stared off at the Senate Buildings at the end of La Rue de Tournon as Hem watched for a taxi. He listened to the sounds of traffic around him and wondered how a man could become a father—twice!— without ever wanting it to happen. The bitterness turned into a harsh laugh at these feelings of dread and this sensation of being unsettled that he couldn't shake off. And then Hem was guiding him into the back seat of a taxi by his elbow and there they were... on their way to fulfill his responsibility as a father.

"She was under the weather when she came back from Egypt," said Ezra. "That's what I thought. Just some exotic flu she'd picked up west of the Nile in Cleopatra country. It never occurred to me that she was pregnant. She's 39 for god's sake!" He laughed the bitter laugh again. "Then she told me when we arrived here in Paris and I've been awfully surrounded by human complications ever since. Can't work. Can't sleep. Can't write."

Hem nodded. "You didn't know she wanted a baby?"

"Well, she may have mentioned it once or twice. But we were always against babies. Wouldn't let anyone bring them to our studio… you remember. Saw what it did even to serious artists when they had one. Not for us, I thought. But then Olga had her baby and I had to go and tell Dorothy."

"Why?"

"It was stupid, I know. But it just felt wrong, her not knowing. I wasn't ashamed, and she knew about Olga, after all."

"But she can't have enjoyed sharing you. You must have known that."

"I guess I did. But she was always so… so damned British about it, though."

"She probably worried that Olga would begin to have more of a hold on you if she bore your child."

"Now that's just stupid."

"You may feel that way now, but over time, I think that would change."

Ezra shook his head impatiently and looked out the window, seeing they were crossing over the Pont Neuf to the Right Bank. What could the driver possibly be thinking? This was a stupid way to go.

* * *

Certificat de Naissance – Omar Shakespear Pound

Omar, du sexe masculine, de Ezra Pound... homme
de lettres, et de Dorothy Shakespear... Dressé le onze
Septembre, mil neuf cent vingt six, seize heures quinze,
sur déclaration du père... Ezra Pound.

* * *

One day previous to that - 10th September 1926 –
Montparnasse, Paris

Ernest wrestled with the sheets and his dark
thoughts all night long in Gerald Murphy's studio in
the Rue Froidevaux, where he'd been staying since the
split with Hadley. He couldn't stop thinking of her, so
cold towards him now and in her own way wrecked by
all this. Or poor little Bumby down in Brittany with the
nanny for the time being so he could fully recover from
his whooping cough, but soon he would come back
home to Paris to find there was no more home and two
separate parents. Or Pauline in her banishment to
Piggott, Arkansas. All this going around in his brain
made the time go so slowly and so horribly and so
flatly that he felt he would have to scream out or gnash
his teeth or break something. The nights were simply
unbelievably terrible.

As soon as the sun was up and light came through
the window, he had to get up and out of there, not even
entirely sure if he'd slept, but finished with lying
prostrated in agonies of the conscience. He felt like a
coffee, but he had been avoiding *La Closerie des Lilas* so

he wouldn't see anyone he knew. Walking along Avenue de Maine one day, he had discovered the *Three Musketeers Café* and had been quietly frequenting it ever since. There he could be alone with his thoughts, which were damn poor company these days, truth be told.

After not too long moping at the café, he decided to go and visit Ezra and Dorothy. He walked in the direction of the Jardin du Luxembourg and forced himself to walk past the Hotel Beauvoir in case he might meet up with Hadley or even just catch a glimpse of her in the window, but he didn't, and it was for the best. He crossed the grounds of the Jardin wondering if he'd bump into Gertrude and Alice out walking their dog. Again, he didn't and again, it was for the best. Their recent disagreement was still too fresh.

He stopped in the lobby of the Hotel Foyot and asked at the front desk if it was a convenient time to call on the Pounds. The desk clerk called up and told Ernest Mrs. Pound would be delighted to see him and that he should hurry. He climbed the stairs and tried to shake the heavy feeling still clinging to him.

Dorothy answered the door looking flushed and holding her pregnant belly.

"Ernest," she said. "Thank god you're here. It's time to go."

"Go where?"

"The hospital. I think I'm having the baby."

"Right now? Where's Ezra?"

"I don't know. Will you take me to the hospital?"

He looked at her, still shocked at this new incarnation of the striking English lady he had known for so many years. Gone was the cool, slim, finely-tailored façade. The dark brown curls were tipped with sweat and the cream complexion was mostly pink now, but she was still a beauty. Hell, he'd been half in love with her since the day he'd met her—even Hadley had remarked on it. Here before him stood a new incarnation: Anglo fertility goddess draped in loose cloth.

"I'd be glad to. Do you need help getting your things together?"

"No, I have it all packed up in that small valise," she said, pointing to a case by the door. "If you could help me down the stairs and see to a taxi that would be lovely."

A pained look came across her face and she grunted and held her breath for a moment before blowing it all out and grabbing for his arm.

"Easy, Dorothy," he said. He picked up the case while holding onto her hand and then guided her towards the door. "Should we send word for Ezra?"

"He won't come," she said simply.

Her breathing was shallow and rapid although her progress down the stairs was slow. She held on tightly to his arm, huffing and puffing at each downward step, always cradling her belly with her other hand. At the bottom of the stairs to the lobby, he called over to the man he'd spoken with before over at the front desk.

"Hello, there," he said. "Aidez-moi, s'il vous plait? Un taxi vite, pour madame. Elle va... having a baby!"

"Le bébé!" said the clerk. He looked at Dorothy. "Oh, mon Dieu! Oui, oui, monsieur. Tout de suite."

A taxi was called for and a chambermaid was summoned. She came out from a back room and began fussing over Dorothy, cooing little pieces of advice and reassurance in her ear. *Asseyez-vous*, Madam.

Lentement. Tous va bien. Restez ici. A chair was brought to the sidewalk for madam to wait for the taxi.

Ernest stood by patiently holding the suitcase and wondering where his friend was in all this. Why wasn't he sticking close to his wife with the baby's arrival imminent? And why had Dorothy said He won't come with such finality? Had something happened between them?

At last, the taxi pulled up and the hotel staff led their patient very carefully to the back seat and gave quick instructions to the driver in French. Ernest tipped the clerk and got in beside Dorothy in the back. The driver pulled away quickly, driving straight up the Rue de Tournon towards the Seine and the Right Bank.

Dorothy was quiet on the drive to the hospital, concentrating on her breathing. They looked out the windows at familiar landmarks and Ernest made a few encouraging comments and held on to her hand for support.

"It'll all be over soon," he said. "And then you'll have this incredible little person to take home with you and a whole new kind of life will begin. You and Ezra will be transformed and it will only bring you closer together, you'll see."

"Oh, we're not bringing the baby home with us," she said.

"You're not?"

"No. We're giving it over to a nurse here in Paris for now and in a year or so it will go over to England to be near my mother. It's all arranged."

"It is?"

She took a deep breath and closed her eyes. "Oh, yes."

"Huh," he said. Didn't know what else to say to that.

91

He might've expected this response from Ezra, but Dorothy? This was a new kind of cold. Where were her maternal feelings? Maybe it would be different when she held her baby in her arms. Or maybe this was the kind of mother Olivia Shakespear had been to her. Was this just the British way of child rearing?

The taxi pulled up at the front of the American Hospital. Ernest looked up at the building and hoped they were close to the Maternity Ward so they wouldn't have far to walk. He picked up the suitcase and stepped out onto the sidewalk.

* * *

Dear Olivia,

I understand you are to become a grandmother at last. Of course, the event is taking place in the usual secrecy. You are probably furious, but you will find a grandchild a pleasing distraction in the end. Congratulations!

Yours,
W.B. Yeats

* * *

Five days before that - 5th September 1926 – Foyot Hotel Restaurant, Paris

Ezra watched his wife devour her second helping of dessert as he sipped his third cup of tea. He resented her appetite and her cheerfulness and their situation, beginning with her pregnancy. But he didn't share this resentment with her and never had. What could he say, when he already had a child with another woman? It's not as though she consulted him before… whenever it happened. When was that? He should know that, shouldn't he? How long had he bounced along here in shock before asking himself that question? Since June.

The waiter stopped by the table to refill their teacups. Dorothy scraped her fork along the surface of her plate to capture the last of the cream filling. He winced.

"Mmm," she said in a half moan, half shiver. "I think I could live on this lemon cake. It is too divine." She put down her fork and sat back in her chair, holding her swollen belly with one hand and reaching for her tea with the other.

"Tell me," said Ezra, leaning forward and putting down his tea cup. "What date did the medicos in Rapallo give you for the blessed event?"

Dorothy looked off to the left above his head and thought for a second. "I can't remember if they gave me an exact date, darling. I think they just said mid-September."

"So if I count backwards nine months, that brings us to mid-December, right?"

"Yes, that's right, I guess."

"But you were in Egypt in mid-December."

"Was I?" she said, squinting at him.

"Yes. You had left Rapallo more than a week before Christmas, because you weren't there when Eliot came for his visit."

"Hmm. I guess I was, then."

93

"So when did this immackalut conception take place? Coz, I don't remember it."

"I guess it must have happened before I left."

"You guess?"

"Well, it must've, musn't it?"

"Not if it happened later."

"That really would be an immaculate conception, wouldn't it?" She laughed without humour, her eyes never leaving his.

"Did it happen later?" He said this steadily, although he was feeling decidedly unsteady.

"I don't know what you mean, darling."

"You know exactly what I mean. You came back from Egypt in March and you were already pregnant, although you just pretended you were feeling sick for a while. My question is simple: did you take a lover when you went to Egypt?"

"Why would you even ask me that? I was home in December and now the baby is due in September. That's nine months, so where's the problem?"

"The problem is I need to know. For my peace of mind. Is the baby mine?"

Her eyes were steady as steel beams and twice as cold, locked onto his face. "Your peace of mind? What about my peace of mind, Ezra? All those years you were seeing the fiddle player so openly, flaunting her to our friends. Letting her sleep in our bed whenever I'm away in England... don't pretend you don't. And then she has your baby. Where's my consolation in all this?"

He rubbed his eyes and tried to stay calm. This is what it was all about right here. "I've never hidden my relationship with Olga from you."

"Oh, well, thank-you very much. That makes it all better, does it? At least we know the paternity of her baby. Or do we? Who's to say she hasn't had a little something on the side in Venice when you're with me in Rapallo? Once an adulteress, always an adulteress, right?"

"Damn it, Dorothy," he said, pounding his fist on the table without meaning to. Several other diners looked their way and he moved his cup and saucer to one side. "Leave it alone. Just answer my simple question: is it mine?"

"If you have to ask me that, then what answer from me is going to set your mind at ease? How could you even trust whatever I told you?"

He put his elbows on the table in front of him and pressed the heels of both hands to his forehead, grinding them into the skin there. "I can't take this, Dorothy. Stop toying with me. It's messing with my mind."

"It's your own mind playing tricks on you, Ezra. It's got nothing to do with me."

Her words were reasonable, but her look was still cold and perhaps a little smug. She was enjoying his discomfort. And that was what finished him.

"I've got to get out of here, Dorothy. I'm going to get a few things from the room and then I'm getting out of this gawd damn hotel. I think you're being an intolerable bitch right now."

She laughed at this.

"I hope you and your baby are happy together," he said, and she never stopped smiling, so he threw his napkin on the table, pushed back his chair and stalked out of the restaurant towards the lobby and the stairs, still feeling a little soapy in his kurranium, but certain he was doing the right thing.

Awkward Stages

About the Author

Happily married since 1992 and a father since 2003, Mark has been a writer for as long as he can remember. He was born in Toronto and grew up in London, Ontario. He was the first winner of the *Lillian Kroll Prize for Creative Writing* at Western University, where he also completed a degree in English Literature. Mark has published novels, poetry, short fiction, feature articles, comic strips and book reviews in various media.

He lives in London with his wife and daughter, those to whom all his work and play is dedicated.

Connect with Mark at his website -
http://markvictoryoung.com/

Praise for the stories:

"Thanks for this potent kick of nostalgia. How important those days were to the adults we've become. Call that 'The High School Theory.'" - Beverly Akerman, author of *The Meaning of Children*

"There are so many good things in this story it's hard to pick one. All I can say is I wish I had written it." - Charles Pinch

Praise for Mark Victor Young's writing:

"A novel which moves along very nicely and captures my attention." – Ann Elizabeth Carson, author of *We all become stories*

"Solid writing with great dialogue and interesting characters!" – Bruce Elgin

"This is the type of book I go to when I want to unwind and forget the world." – Lucy Butler

"That voice makes us curious and keeps us reading."
– Cynthia Dagnal-Myron

Publication History:

Crotch Dogs was originally published by
CommuterLit.com as of 18th June 2012.

Fault Lines was originally published on
CommuterLit.com as of 20th May 2014.

Frank's Wager was originally published in Issue
Number 7 of *The Writers Block,* on 10th January 2011.

The Tree House was originally published on
CommuterLit.com on 6th July 2011.

Practical Uses of Voodoo in the Workplace originally
appeared on Litro.co.uk on 13th January 2013.

Ezra and Ernest originally appeared on
CommuterLit.com on 9th December 2014.

Also from *Hanton House* by Mark Victor Young
***Risk* - a Novel**

They're the most unlikely detectives.

Martin is a 38-year-old virgin marked for greatness by the insurance gods. In his professional life, he is paid to assess risk, but in his personal life he plays it safe. Experience has shown him that lonely is better than broken-hearted.

George is a wannabe architect with white man's dreadlocks. He risks his neck on the streets of Toronto every day as a bike courier, but his job is unchallenging and he chooses apathy over the risk of failure at what he really wants to do.

When George tags along with Martin to investigate the scene of his latest claim, they stumble upon a burglary in process. Now they are being hunted by an unknown adversary who will stop at nothing to get what he's after, forcing Martin and George into a dangerous game of cat and mouse in which they must risk everything.

Sample First Chapter

Martin Porchnik could see Jason from Claims approaching the Underwriting area with a yellow file in his hand and a big smirk on his face. A chill went through Martin, as it always did. A yellow file meant a property claim to be paid, and although he would ask not for whom the bell tolled, he still prayed it didn't toll for he.

"Good afternoon, 'Underwear' department. Whose day can I ruin today?" said Jason. "Anybody have a file for Ultimate Diecasting?"

Martin grimaced. He knew that name. Of all the shit files that landed in his lap, that one stuck out in his memory as one of the shittiest.

"Heads are going to roll over this one," said Jason, looking around with an evil grin.

"Not one of mine," said Darlene.

"It's not me," called Dave from his cubicle at the back.

"It's me," said Martin. Everybody looked at him and he shrugged his shoulders. What're ya gonna do?

"Is this the kind of crap you're writing down here?" Jason parked his bulk next to Martin's desk, leaning his elbow on the upper shelf. "No wonder I'm so busy paying out the big bucks. I need a dec page, underwriter boy."

He was what might be called a *big galoot*. Tallish and stocky going on fat with dark curly hair and thick eyebrows that looked angry or at least sarcastic all the time and a kind of goatee that made him look devilish.

"I haven't even issued the policy, yet," Martin said, looking away from Jason's dark eyes and back down at the yellow file that spelled possible doom. Did he have to enjoy it so much?

"Well, what's the hold up? Let's get it in gear. Do I have to come down here and crack the whip on you people?"

"It just came in last week." He dug through his pile of bound submissions waiting to be entered into the computer.

"Well, that didn't take long. What have you got for me, so I know how much I have to pay out here? Or did you want me to just give them a blank check?"

"We have a copy of their last year's dec page from the prior carrier. We bound coverage on the same basis." Well, he hadn't, but his boss had. The decs, or policy declarations, which were a listing of the coverages and wordings included, had just landed in his lap, in fact. And right away he had to hand them over to Jason so he could pay the first claim. Delightful.

"Gee, thanks. I guess it's something to go by. I'll make a copy, then."

"Can you leave me the claim file?"

"Sure. Read it and weep." Jason passed him the file and then walked away to the mail room to make his photocopy.

"Believe me, there will be tears," said Martin. He opened the file with a small feeling of self-satisfaction that he hoped wouldn't show on his face. He wasn't the one who had put them on the risk, so the blame wouldn't fully fall to him, come to that. It gave him a little get-out-of-jail-free card, but it was something he had to pretend he didn't think.

Underwriters spend most of every day considering risk. They read submissions of potential "risks," which in his department were businesses they were asked to insure. They had to assess the likelihood of having to pay out money because of some misadventure that might befall each. This would be some kind of lawsuit or a fire or a flood, etc. If you included famine, you would have almost all four horsemen of the Apocalypse. War is excluded. Underwriters choose which businesses to insure and how much money to charge so that, on average, a certain class of business would make money for the company.

The general principle of insurance is that the premiums of the many pay for the losses of the few. So they wrote up business for a whole lot of machine shops across Canada and only a few, like Ultimate Diecasting, would have a claim, and it should all even out and whatever was left over minus expenses was profit. If Martin did his job right.

So that is most of what underwriters do: consider which risks to get and which ones to keep by renewing. The rest of what they do all day is worry that the risks they have selected will have a big claim and they will be hauled onto the mat to answer for it. Consider risk and worry for a living. Nice work if you can get it. Martin shook his head and tried to concentrate on the claim report.

The date of loss was Sunday, so it had been the previous night. It was a professional hit. The line to the alarm monitoring station had been cut and the bars had been taken out along with the window, which was removed in one piece from the frame. The place was a mess and the only things missing were plans and blueprints from a current job. There would be a payout under "Valuable Papers" and a Business Interruption loss while the plans were reassembled. They would have to pay to have the line repaired and the window replaced. Nothing else stolen or destroyed. That didn't sound right.

This one had disaster written all over it from the start. He remembered when the phone call had come in from the broker, only a week ago, and it hadn't passed the sniff test from the start.

"Hi, Martin. Listen, I've got a piece of new business for you. It's a machine shop. Do you think you could do it for four thousand bucks?"

"Let me take a look at it. Put some details on paper and fax it over."

"Can't you just quote me over the phone?"

"Well, what do they make?"

"Just various metal products."

"It makes a difference to what we would charge. And I'll also need construction and protection details on the building to determine the property rate."

"It's HCB, steel deck roof, of course. What else? I'm a busy man, Martin. I don't have time to get into all this detail."

"I can't quote over the phone. I'll need something in writing. Including receipts. Do they sell to the U.S.?"

"What do you think? Everybody sells to the U.S. This is just a little risk, I don't see the big deal."

"Sales to the U.S. increases our exposure. You'd better send something over."

"I'll get back to you."

Unbelievable, was his first thought when he had hung up the phone. What do we even need underwriters for if that's the way we're going to deal in insurance? It's not about the size of the building they occupy, or the number of people they have working for them, their level of training and qualification, or who they sell their products to, or how much they sell, or how much equipment they have and what it costs to replace it, would a key piece of equipment shut down the whole shop while it was being repaired, or whether they deal in cash or credit, or how long a fire would put them out of business, or ten or fifty other things that Jed Johansen wouldn't think to ask... it's about a few thousand bucks and a quick sale. Granted, 99% of brokers were diligent and professional and trustworthy, but it was the ones like Jed Johansen that you had to watch or else you ended up in situations like the one he was currently facing.

Jed never did send in a full quote submission, he just went over Martin's head and spoke to Gerry. "Gerry" was short for Geraldine, his supervisor. She preferred the diminutive, as she didn't live in the Victorian age. She was tall and confident and blond, and Martin found her easier to deal with than his previous boss. She had an intelligent face and sharp eyes. She was impatient all the time, but kind. From looking at the pictures on the desk of her husband and kids, he imagined she was one of those busy moms who were great with their kids, efficient at work and able to keep the whole world spinning on the end of a stick.

"I just got off the phone with one of the Johansen brothers, I forget which," Gerry had said when she dropped by his desk not twenty minutes after the first phone call came through. "I bound that risk, the machine shop, for $5000. He's faxing over last year's dec page."

"Oh," he had said hesitantly. This was very bad form, indeed. Without a written submission, there were no declarations or representations from the broker upon which to rely, and as they say, a verbal contract isn't worth the paper it's printed on, ha-ha.

"I know," said Gerry. "You're not happy about it."

Martin shrugged but looked steadily at her. "Not really. I don't like him bypassing me to get to you. You can't be doing all the quotes in the department."

"I know. It was an accommodation. This is a growth year, and we have got to take it where we can get it. Besides, we can get it inspected and take care of any problems then."

"When it will be too late to get more premium if we need it."

"It'll be fine, Martin. Besides, we're $5K to the good, instead of nothing, and I want to switch the Johansens on so they'll start sending us more business."

"I understand."

Five thousand dollars? They knew nothing about security, products, contracts, warranties... it would have to be inspected, thought Martin, just as the fax had been dropped off in his IN box.

It was out in Scarberia, their nickname for Scarborough, the north east part of Toronto. It was in a moderately high crime area, big limits on tools and computers, which were the first to go. This was terrible. The Total Insured Value, or TIV, was over $4 million: the company's money on the line for who knows what. And now a claim, proving him right about his fears.

"Here's your so-called dec page back." Jason loomed by his desk again. "Can I have my file back, or were you going to take it home with you?"

"It's all yours. Why do you think thieves would break into a place like that and not steal any tools or computers? Things with a quick turn around. Those are usually the first to go, and yet these thieves ignored them."

"What do you think, oh brainy one?"

"I think they knew what they were looking for. All they took was highly specialized diagrams, plans, and design specs. What petty thief takes that?"

"Okay, so what?"

"It sounds suspicious, that's all. I think you should be careful with this one. It's bothered me since we wrote it."

"Well, thanks for the advice. I'm glad you know so much about how to do my job, because you obviously didn't know how to do yours."

"Hey, it was just a suggestion."

"I'll take it under advisement," said Jason over his shoulder.

When the adjuster had left, Martin quickly composed a fax form and fired it off to the broker: *Urgent. Insist that the insured upgrades security system to provide ULC-approved Line Security Level III protection, to prevent a recurrence of this kind of loss. Please advise ASAP how the insured intends to proceed. Our file is in abeyance pending your reply.* Then he walked over and knocked on Gerry's door.

"I know what you're going to say. I heard about it."

"I'm not going to say anything. I'm just wondering about this loss. It sounds suspicious to me. No tools or computers stolen. I still don't think we've got the whole story here, and that could mean non-disclosure. In which case we could VOID the policy *ab initio*."

"Marty. Get a grip. Bad losses happen to good underwriters. It's not your fault, and I know that. Leave the investigation to the Claims Department."

"Okay. I faxed the broker to get the line security in

there or else face the hammer."

"That's all we can do. Now blow it off. You've had bigger losses than this. Besides, it builds character."

"It builds my stress level is what it does."

Leaving Gerry to her managing, he returned to his cube feeling dissatisfied. It was a mystery, that was for sure. But if he were reading this mystery in one of his detective novels, he would've put it down by now. Too boring. Something about this was not right, but it wasn't really his place to intrude. Let the Claims Department do their work. They were thorough, Jason's bluster notwithstanding. If there was something to find, they'd find it. Time to shake this off with a little caloric input.

He sat in the lunchroom quietly munching his sandwich. People came and went, mostly going back to eat at their desks, or going out for lunch. Martin was a fixture in the lunchroom: same time, same lunch, everyday. Lunch was about giving his mind a break. No magazines or TV, no conversation, no stimuli. It wasn't a Zen thing: be the sandwich, one hand clapping, or whatever. It just felt good to decompress and not think about anything, if he could manage it. Concentrate on the flavor of the sandwich and the chocolate bar.

It was the chocolate bars that gave him the spare tire, he felt, but he couldn't stop. They were an addiction. He was about 5'10", pudgy, especially around the gut. The old hairline was slowly retreating on him. At 38 years old, this was right on schedule, par for the genetic course. Thanks, Grandpa. But it didn't help that the media was always bombarding women with images of the ideal male, an ideal he couldn't live up to. Calvin Klein underwear ads had set his self-esteem back a pace, he could admit it now.

He poured another cup of coffee and went back to the cube. He tried to get back into the flow of things, but the stupid loss kept bugging him and he ended up just staring off into space for long periods of time, just trying to crack the code of this puzzle. That was how George, the bicycle courier who did their head office mail run every day found him, lost in thought at his desk.

"Hey, buddy," he said, picking up the name plate on his desk and flipping it over in his hand, tapping it on the desk. "Where's my envelope?"

"Hey, go easy on the name plate."

"Sorry about that. I don't want to break the last link to your sense of identity."

"Don't worry, my name's sewn into the backs of all my shirts."

"There you go. You'll be fine."

"All right, just let me collect it up." Martin got up out of his chair, glad for something else to think about and a chance to shoot the breeze with George. He had been doing the pick-ups at their office for a few years now and he and Martin had been out for drinks a couple of times after work. He was a good guy, despite his scary appearance. Tall, sunglasses, white man's dreadlocks, tattoos, pierced this and that... he wasn't like Martin's insurance friends, but that's what he liked about him. He was different.

"No rush. I'm ahead of schedule today," said George.

George came with him into the mail room, and talked to him as he gathered up all the envelopes, memos, and various other correspondence, packaged and weighed it all, and wrote out the receiving slip.

"So, rough day, or just hungry?" said George.

"It's been one of those days. Started out okay, but it all went quickly downhill this afternoon."

"Sounds like a pretty normal Monday."

"Yeah, I guess. Well, here it is. Signed, sealed, and now just to be delivered."

"Thanks. We going for drinks tonight, Marty?"

"Not tonight, but maybe some night this week."

"Just say the word." George put on his sunglasses as Martin walked him out through the office and over to the main door.

"Bye, George," called Janice.

"Bye." The door closed behind him.

"Whew, he's cute," said Janice. "Do you know if he's single?"

"Um, yes. I mean, yes, I do know he lives with his girlfriend."

"Too bad. Such a hottie! He can deliver my package anytime."

Janice was a bit of a hottie herself, in that secretary way. Single secretaries exude this air of availability and eagerness, like bridesmaids. She was no supermodel, which Martin didn't mind. That type of woman intimidated Martin, anyway. They always looked so severe, so hard, with angry-looking cheek bones. He always imagined them as martial arts experts, capable of knocking his block off if he so much as looked at them.

No, she was solidly built, pretty, and seemed fun to be around. Shoulder length blond hair-product hair, small features, fair-sized bust and hips. Looking very fertile. In her early 30's, he guessed. But she would probably say no. Look at him. Why would she go out with him? He wasn't much to look at. And even if they did go out once or twice, something would happen and the whole thing would go to hell and it would hurt like the last time he got involved with someone. Then he wouldn't be able to look her in the eye at work the next morning. Always have to pretend to check out the paint job on the walls as he walked by her desk. And face the shame of a failed office romance. It wasn't worth it.

Quietly back across the office, shy glance around, wishing he could turn himself invisible, wanting to escape people's notice and make it back to the safety of his little cube without anyone confronting him. Feeling strangely persecuted, as if everyone were against him. Couldn't seem to face anything or anyone right now.

--

For further details or to purchase a copy of *Risk*, please visit http://markvictoryoung.com/risk/.

Also from *Hanton House* by Mark Victor Young
***Once Were Friends* - a Novel**

If you think it's hard to win back the one that got away,
try doing it while you're taking over her family's company.

To save the firm his father built, ambitious CEO **Hal Mercer** has to initiate a hostile takeover of industry giant D'Arville Industries.

Owned by the family of the only woman he's ever loved, **Kate D'Arville** certainly isn't going to stand by and let him destroy her family's empire. If only she'd have dinner with him, he could make her understand his intentions. If Hal fails, it's his family's company that's doomed, his employees who'll lose their jobs. He can't let that happen, but Hal isn't used to having everyone counting on him like this.

Problem is, it's becoming less clear which is more important to him — winning the corporate battle of his life or the heart of the woman he loves.

Sample First Chapter

They were pinned down under heavy fire in the empty shell of what had looked like a partially burned-out general store. Hal Mercer crouched below a windowless frame on the second floor, listening for footsteps on the stairs. *Damn! Now his mask was fogging up.* He tried to wipe it with one finger, hearing shouts in the smoky air as the enemy crawled up their unprotected flank, the heavy *Phut! Phut! Phut!* of sniper fire covering their approach. Where the hell did he go from here?

Hal glanced out the window. Abandoned car wrecks covered with spray paint lined the street in front of the building, stacks of tires lay toppled at the curb, obscure suggestions of movement over there told him that enemy positions were advancing along the tree line to his right, and then the sound of two slugs slamming into the window frame next to his ear made him duck back under the ledge. Raising his gun over the ledge for a moment, he squeezed off a round in the general direction of the trees.

"Archie?" he shouted off into the darkness to his left.

"Yes, *mon capitaine?*"

"You see those guys coming up by the trees?"

A pause. "Yes, sir."

"Can you create a diversion on your side to draw their fire?"

"I'm on the case, sir."

Archie was playing some kind of game, obviously. He wasn't this good at taking orders and he also hated Hal intensely. He would be more likely to stab Hal in the back than cover it for him.

"Go ahead, then," Hal yelled.

Then a shuffling noise from the next room and several shots followed by a wet *SLAP*, and Archie Bishop's voice shouting, "I'm hit, I'm hit! They got me, captain!"

Hal's heart was pounding in his chest as he reviewed his options. With Archie out, he was likely all alone here on the second floor, with who knew how many of his division gone. Going outside would be suicide, as he could see from the figures advancing on all sides, but staying here only delayed the inevitable.

Then there was a squeak from behind him, and the sound of a careful footstep on the stairs, and Hal, keeping low under the window, crawled to the darkened corner at the far end of the room, his weapon pointed at the top of the stairs. The dark shape of a head bobbed into view, eyes trained along the barrel of a gun that scanned left and right like a periscope on an emerging submarine. Then more of the body came into view: an absurdly tall, hunched-over figure with sticking-out ears and ridiculous fatigues—it was Johnson from Accounting.

"Die, pencil-pusher," said Hal as he squeezed the trigger, firing a single round into Johnson's midsection.

"Ow!" said Johnson. "I'm hit."

The adrenaline rush was amazing! Oh, well. Nothing left to lose. Hal scurried to the window and started firing at anything and everything that moved. "Banzai! This one's for Archie." He caught someone hurrying across the street in front of him and quickly fired a couple of rounds in that direction. A woman's voice called out, "I'm hit," just as he caught sight of the tiny yellow orb coming at him, seemingly growing larger as it descended along its shallow arc, and exploding on contact with his visor. Shaking his head from the surprising force of the impact, he couldn't quite shake off the darkness of the thick paint obscuring his view.

Hal shouted, "I'm hit," and sank back blindly onto the floor to wait for the whistle. He had been killed yet again, but he couldn't help smiling. Who knows what it was doing for morale, but he was having the most fun he'd had in ages. Why had it taken him so long to discover the joy of paint ball? He felt good about the way the Senior Management team rallied around him, even if they had lost two of their three engagements. What the heck, at worst it was something different for everyone to do on a weekend that was on the company tab.

Okay, sure, he wasn't that "easy come, easy go" about it. He had spent weeks planning this event and was desperately hoping everyone was having fun. And morale simply had to improve; it couldn't get much worse. It was a tough time for the company now and if he was going to achieve what he wanted—no, scratch that—what he had to achieve, then he had to make some changes for the better.

Was he the only one who worried about this stuff?

Right. Sniff, sniff. It's lonely at the top.

* * *

"Okay, troops. Let's bring it in," said Bill Fluellen, the section manager, as they were milling around in the lobby. Pete Malden rolled his eyes. Another management speech. Didn't he get enough of this during the work week? He looked over at Fluellen. His boss was an imposing figure even when he wasn't dressed in military fatigues. His thick red hair and salt and paprika goatee was flecked with sweat and sawdust.

"We did great out there," he was saying. "We worked together and really stuck it to those wallies from the IT crew. Malden and Bardolph, way to cover each other. Where's Bardolph?"

"Right here, sir. Ten-hut!" Randy Bardolph snapped to attention behind his boss in a mock salute.

"At ease. You were quite the drama queen with your little 'death scene' out there."

"Sorry, sir. Next time I give up my life for you in battle, I'll try to go with more dignity."

"Excellent. Bottom line, we came together as a team and defended our position despite overwhelming odds. As your commanding officer, I was damn proud to lead you onto the field. That's the last exercise of the day, so I'll just say enjoy the rest of your weekend, and I'll see you back at the office Monday morning."

Pete sat on a low bench against the wall and covered his nose with his sleeve as the pervasive combined aroma of stale sweat, cigar smoke and something moldy mingled with the fresh body odors filling the room. Randy, Amy, and Arthur sat or stood next to him.

"Pete, I love the blue hair," said Amy, smoothing her own hair behind both ears with her fingertips. "You should really keep it like that." Her dark hair was in a short bob kept away from her face. She had a mostly slim and petite frame, so her navy sweatshirt with the George Brown College logo hung a bit too loosely from her shoulders, but her curvy hips filled out her dark olive army pants so she didn't just look skinny.

He liked being able to see this casual side of her. Even on dress down day she wasn't like this, preferring business casual to jeans and a T-shirt. Those army pants were driving him wild. He wondered if they could somehow make paint ball a weekly thing.

Pete caught her eye and then ran his fingers through the blue patch of hair and looked away. "Yeah, thanks. My version of a battle scar. 'It's a far better thing I do than I have ever done', one life to give for the department and all that."

"So what are we supposed to feel now? A stronger sense of team cohesion?" said Randy. "Or do you find yourself with even more questions about the people you work with?"

"Yeah," said Arthur. "Like what was with those IT geeks who had their own guns?"

"Scary," said Pete. "And some were like automatics or something."

"I have a picture in my mind," said Randy, applying two fingers to his right temple and closing his eyes, his mouth pursed in a little smirk. He was what you might call portly, but with a dignified air and busy hands with long fingers that were animated when he talked and drumming or tapping when he was listening. He cleared his throat. "They are here every weekend, keeping track of their 'kill-shots,' have a full set of military fatigues—no offence, Amy—have no girlfriends, live in their parents' basements which smell exactly like this place, and they're each composing the ultimate online game to ensure their places in history."

Amy put a hand on her hip. "The only reason I have these army pants is because they were in fashion for about 10 minutes when I was in grade 12, and this is the only place I've had a chance to wear them since then, and when's the last time you had a girlfriend, Randy?"

"Touché," said Randy.

"I think you make a cute military chick," said Pete.

"Thank-you, Peter." She smiled at him.

"Yeah, I was going to say that, too, Amy," said Arthur. "I noticed the same thing."

Pete looked at his rival. Shit, that's all he needed. Not that Arthur was much competition. He was tall and thin with a generally hunched posture that looked a bit like he was trying to brace himself for impact. Inexplicably, he was wearing a blue oxford cloth button down and beige cotton chinos, as if he were off to a college mixer of yesteryear, albeit they were now tie-dyed with paint splotches. Did they have college mixers in the Summer of Love?

Amy gave Arthur a suspicious look. "There's no way I'm doing your reconciliation for you next week so you can forget it."

"No, I wouldn't, I just…" said Arthur.

Randy patted Arthur on the shoulder. "Of course you wouldn't, Arthur. Did anybody catch sight of our fearless leader? He was supposed to be here today."

"Hal? No, but I would love to know who shot him," said Pete.

"We'll hear about it Monday, I'm sure," said Amy.

"I'm surprised we didn't get a speech from the little general," said Randy.

"Which unit just squared off with the S&M team?" asked Arthur, using their secret code for the Senior Management group.

"I think it was Marketing, and you know they'd lie down and play dead rather than smoke the big bosses," said Pete, leaning back against the wall and folding his arms across his chest. "They know which side their bread is buttered." He had a slim build and wore black jeans and a long sleeve red t-shirt with a Spider-Man symbol surrounded by webs on the front. His blue eyes and long lashes were the occasional envy of the women in his life, but his normally dark and not blue hair was short and messy-on-purpose.

"They're smart. You've got to learn to play politics with the management types if you ever want to become one." Amy made a nose plugging gesture and craned her neck to see over the crowd. "Geez, it smells. Is that line getting any shorter? I'd really like to get out of here."

"I know," said Pete. "I feel like the smell is in my mouth now. I might just need a cold beer to counteract it."

* * *

"So whose idea was it to do this whole team-building paint ball thing, anyway?" said Arthur as they sat around a table at *The Fletcher's Quiver* Pub. They had a booth to the right of the bar, slightly toward the back. Pete surveyed the room and the various Robin Hood artifacts above their heads.

"Well, what else can you think of that's new around the office?" said Randy.

"Yeah, I know Hal is the new CEO, but do you really think it was his idea?"

"Of course it is. When you're the new guy, you have to come in and piss on the bushes, mark your territory," said Randy. "This is just one of many new things still to come, and not all of them will be good, just wait."

"But it was his father's company," said Arthur. "Why would he want to change things so much? I mean, doesn't that reflect poorly on his dad?"

"More likely he wants it to reflect well on him," said Pete.

"Yes, our boy does have a reputation to live down," said Randy. "He was the biggest shit disturber of all of us when he worked the floor with Pete and me."

"Wow," said Arthur.

Randy and Pete exchanged an uncomfortable glance, remembering somebody was missing. A year earlier, they would have been here with Hal, talking about the very people he was probably out for drinks with right now.

Thursday nights after work were what Hal had dubbed "group therapy" sessions at the local watering hole. There were always five to ten of them from the office, a revolving door of old pros, new hires who looked promising and the core group of Hal, Pete and Randy. Hal would get Randy going about something and then he would hold court while Hal bought a round of *B-52s* or *Sexes on the Beach* or something and hit on the waitresses. Pete would draw pictures of the senior managers or supervisors and they would end up eating chicken wings for their dinner around 10 o'clock and then close out the bar. Pete and Randy would stumble onto the subway and Hal would grab a taxi going the other way, often with female companionship in tow.

For about the last six months it had been just Pete and Randy. After Arthur had joined their section, he had come out once in a while, but their get-togethers had become less frequent since Hal had ascended the top of the org chart. The dynamic was somewhat flat without him.

"Yeah," said Pete. "And before he surprised everyone and came to work with us, he did the whole life of leisure, rich kid, country club. We heard all the stories, believe me."

Randy nodded agreement while he finished a sip of his martini. "My uncle golfed at his club and knew him well. Hal would spend all day on the golf course. An excellent golfer, I'm told."

"I'll bet he was a hit with the ladies," said Amy. "With that rock star hair and those dark eyes… mmm, yummy."

"You have a woody for our CEO?" said Pete. "Ewww. Now I know how you plan to get to the top."

"He can heighten my, um, future prospects any time." Amy smiled at all of them.

"Quite," said Randy. "But you notice the rock star hair was gone before the board meeting when they voted on his coronation? And he actually went out and bought his first suit. Our boy Hal has really grown up."

"I'm sure he had his suit and haircut before the funeral," said Pete. The others all nodded and found it was a good time to have a sip of their drinks and inspect their surroundings. Pete looked down at the Robin Hood caricature he'd been doodling on a spare bar mat, picked it up and shook it to dry the ink. "But I'll give you this: he was the laziest one of any of us on the fifteenth floor."

"Hear, hear," said Randy. He looked at his watch. "Well, I think it's time I moved on. Do you still need a ride?" He touched Arthur's arm.

"Yeah," said Arthur, sucking back the last of his beer.

Randy indicated the half full glasses in front of them. "Are you guys staying on?"

"I'm just going to finish this beer," said Pete.

"Me, too," said Amy.

"Right. See you Monday." Randy waved and walked to the front door and out, followed closely by Arthur.

Pete smiled and had a casual sip of his drink. "Sorry, I didn't mean to break up the party."

"You didn't," said Amy. "It was just one of those pauses in the conversation. And I think Randy was realizing he sounded a little full of himself."

"Doesn't he always?"

"Let's see how you're coming along with Robin Hood. Hey, pretty good likeness of Hal, there. Is he an anti-Robin? The rich stealing from the poor?"

"Isn't that what the rich always do? No, I just felt like putting his head on a Robin Hood body. Inspired by my surroundings."

Amy nodded. "It's really good."

"Thanks. So what did you think of today, really?"

"I liked it. As corny as it sounds, it does build team spirit. It lets us have a little fun and see a different side of the people we work with, and I would never have tried it otherwise."

"Yeah, I guess so. But requiring us to give up most of our Saturday for a work function kinda bugs me."

"I work plenty of Saturdays as it is."

"Yeah, but that's different. It's voluntary. I don't know, it just rubs me the wrong way. Do I really want to socialize with the people I work with? Don't I see them enough with, what, 45% of my waking hours spent at work already?"

"Should I be offended?"

"I didn't mean you, and you know it."

"Hey, you could've got a doctor's note."

"I know. Ignore me, I'm just lipping off. So what do you have planned for tonight? Any hot date on the horizon?"

"A hot date with my laundry is all."

"What, no boyfriend for the great Amy Quick, after giving Randy a hard time this afternoon over his lack of female companionship?"

"I don't think Randy craves female companionship. And no, neither of us has a boyfriend."

"Whaaat? You think Randy's gay? Just because he doesn't have a girlfriend? Does that make me gay, too?"

"No, with you I can't see it. But Randy has a quality, as they say." She paused and looked towards the door. "He never really talks about his social life, does he?"

"I, let me think... Who did he go on vacation with that time? Down south?"

"My point exactly. A friend is all he said."

"All right, maybe. I don't know. So what if he is?"

"I just like to ride him a little bit. See if I can shake his unflappable reserve."

"But you're not going to cause any embarrassing scenes? I prefer 'don't ask, don't tell,' if we could just keep it at that."

"Oh, I'm not going to out him, don't worry. Now what have you drawn there?"

"Oh, this." He shook the bar mat dry again and showed her the second figure.

She took it and peered at it while holding it to face the light. "What is that? Is that Randy as a cat?"

"That's Randy as a player in Cats."

"Oh, I get it. A Broadway musical." She smiled and put it back down on the table.

"Yes, I guess you've poisoned my mind now, and I will never be able to think of him without thinking that."

"You know what they say about homophobes…"

"No, I don't. And I don't want to know. Not that I think that way. I'm fine with it."

Amy nodded and sipped her drink down to the ice cubes.

"So what happened with, I think his name was Joey, or Joe?"

"What?"

"The old boyfriend? Now no longer."

"Oh, yeah. Well, I guess we were both so busy with work, we were just seeing each other less and less. I'm still doing the night school classes, so it was hard to even get a free night that we could get together. So I said let's quit it and save ourselves a painful break-up."

"Right. That's grounds for a painful break-up right there."

"He was okay. Relieved, almost. We both realized it wasn't going anywhere, I think."

"You think."

"You don't know Joe. He works longer hours than I do."

"Mmm."

"Well, it's getting to be that time." She looked around for a clock. "My dirty clothes beckon."

"Yeah, I guess I'll get going, too. Where are you parked?" He shimmied down to the end of the bench and stood.

"Right out front," she said, standing. "Where are you?"

"Not far." They walked around the front of the bar and out the main door to the sidewalk. Pete pointed back down the road towards the *Paint War!* building. "Back the way we came. About a block back, there. The red one."

"Okay, well, see you Monday." She smiled and squinted into the light.

"See you Monday. Right." He did a sort of wave, and half turned towards his car.

Amy produced a key fob from her purse and aimed it at a car, pressing a button that made the car's lights flash. She walked around to the driver's side and opened the door. "Bye."

He nodded. "Bye."

Pete walked down the sidewalk towards his car, not looking back in case she was watching to see if he looked back. No more boyfriend. This was fantastic. He hadn't lied about her military outfit—he was hot for her in those clothes. He had, of course, always noticed her tight little body and always felt a bit of the tease in the way she looked at him and talked to him. Now that there was no boyfriend in the picture, it was all about strategy. Time to make his move. He would have to deal with Arthur, of course, but that would wait until Monday.

It was a cool fall day, slightly overcast. He drove home with the windows down and his music turned up, smiling at nothing. Home was a one-bedroom apartment in the Danforth, Toronto's Greektown area. It was sparsely furnished, had a cabinet full of movies, and everywhere boxes and boxes of comics. Various framed superhero posters by his favorite artists decorated the walls.

The kitchen table was also his drawing board for his

own drawings, most of which were of the superhero or heroine variety. His Saturday night consisted of a heated can of ravioli eaten at the table while working on a large-scale Batman scene, with the original Batman movie, the one with Jack Nicholson as The Joker, playing in the background for atmosphere.

There used to be more furniture, and some throw pillows, and tasteful decorative prints on the walls, and no room for any of his things in the bathroom, but that stuff had been gone for some time now. Now there was more room for his comics, and he could leave the boxes all over the place and no one complained.

At the same time, he missed the other stuff.

--

For further details or to purchase a copy of *Once Were Friends*, please visit http://markvictoryoung.com/once-were-friends/

Coming soon from Mark Victor Young
The Launch - **a novel**

Watson Sinclair has only been in New York for a
couple of hours and already he's had a small accident
in his car involving some distracting cleavage and an
inconveniently-placed fruit stand. His best friend **JC
Dubois** is a few blocks away, kidnapping the editor of
the Royal Features Syndicate. Watson has to pick them
up and they have to get back across the Canadian
border safely with their prisoner. It didn't have to be
this way.

Watson and JC always wanted to be cartoonists for
the daily papers. Their dreams came true when they
received a syndication contract for their comic strip.
But then months went by and legendary editor Ray
Bennett stopped returning their calls. They were faced
with a choice: give up and go back to their day jobs or
consider drastic measures to get the job done. Like
kidnapping Ray and taking over the launch of the strip
themselves.

The plan is simple: drive to New York to take Ray
and his laptop back to London. Give orders to Ray's
prick of an Assistant Editor. Keep Ray quiet and
secure, convince his staff that he is working from home

and keep all this from their wives. They've got one week.

If they pull this off and execute a successful launch, their dreams are back on track. If they screw it up and get caught, they go to jail. Nothing like a little motivation.

Sample Chapter

My name is Watson Sinclair and I am a pathetically heterosexual man. Not the kind who decides in elementary school that he likes girls but is too shy to do anything about it all the way through high school graduation, learning what he can from teen romance books, pornography and playground rumors, although that, too. Compulsive ogling is the true symptom of my condition and unsubtle rubbernecking its unfortunate result. I have always lived in fear that I would see some particularly attractive woman while driving and be so distracted that I'd just drive my car up onto the sidewalk, probably uncorking a fire hydrant or something. This has never happened to me until now.

The particularly attractive woman who has so completely bamboozled my powers of concentration is radically under-dressed for the weather and is probably running across the street from her office or something. Tight black skirt, black tights and long spiky heels in the snow, but no coat. She has long dark hair, creamy skin flushed from the cold and a low-cut shirt with excellent cleavage, but as I'm realizing that I have run up into a sidewalk fruit stand, she's turning a corner and now there's a Korean guy yelling at me and waving a broom.

What is even sicker than forgetting you are driving a car to stare at a woman who hasn't given you the slightest provocation is that seeing all this fruit on the ground, I can't help thinking that her boobs are at least as big as these large navel oranges, maybe even the grapefruits. And speaking of headlights, I've got no time to sit around picking citrus out of my grill. I was only supposed to drive around the block a few times and come back and now this damn calamity.

I peel off a couple of twenties and drop them on top of the pile of fruit in the snow. I jump back in the front seat, slamming and then locking the door just as the broom hits home on the window. Thank God the front of the car was nose deep in wooden stalls or he'd have come at me straight instead of having to circle around the back. I give him a polite wave and smile even though his spittle is flecking my window as he shouts incoherently. And all this because I am a goggle-eyed tongue loller who can't look away from T&A. Normally I rely on my best friend and artistic partner, JC Dubois, to say "Eyes on the road, Watson," but he is currently a few blocks away, kidnapping the Editorial Director of the Royal Features Syndicate.

I honk my horn and pull back into traffic. Yes, I'm Canadian and a crazy driver: deal with it. It has to be the stress of driving in this metropolitan mayhem that short-circuited my brain into looking for some comforting eye candy like that office hottie. Focus, Watson. I'm in Midtown near the park and I have to get back to the Royal Features building. I drove past the MOMA two blocks ago and I got stuck in traffic for a while, then I saw Carnegie Hall at one point. If I can make it there, I know I can get back to where I started. Damn these Manhattan one way streets. I can't stop to ask for directions, because I just know some hilarious New Yorker will say "Practice," when I ask how to get to Carnegie Hall.

Speaking of Big Apple clichés straight out of a Woody Allen film, there are yellow taxis just everywhere. I think they see the Ontario plates and jump all over me like a lion on a gazelle. I hate to think what their insurance rates must look like, because I have stomped on the binders more times in the last five minutes than I have since my renewal. If JC texts me right now I'm in trouble. Finally, there's an oldster asleep at the switch. Muscle the nose of the car into this small gap, cue honking, now flip him the bird while inching into the space I've created. There. I'm moving again and the old guy is back there miming the "storm on the heath" scene from King Lear. Man, he is *coming apart*. I guess you get used to this eventually.

Through a patch of daylight between buildings I can see the Rockefeller Center, which means Fifth Avenue is coming up. I'm on East 55th Street heading west, which sounds strange, but I know this will get me back to Seventh Avenue, which will get me down to Carnegie Hall. We went over these maps fifty times, it feels like, and thank God we did. Traffic is actually moving along a bit, so I'm in good position. What is taking JC so long?

The last time either of us planned and executed a crime was when we were twelve. We ran a complicated distraction technique whereby JC asked the shopkeeper how much were the dusty boxes of 35mm film up on a high shelf and I swiftly pocketed two chocolate bars and exited the store. We felt guilty about it in the parking lot afterward because the guy who ran the store was really nice and that was the end of our career as criminals. Until now.

As I'm changing lanes to turn right onto Seventh Avenue, I hear a bicycle bell chiming at me urgently. This is it. I pick up my cell phone just to confirm he's ready for pickup.

The eagle has landed.

That JC. Always quick with a book reference. I didn't think my adrenal system could work any harder. My out-of-province medical would cover a heart attack, but it would really slow us down right now. I make the turn onto Seventh and hurry up and wait for the light. Come on green, I know you can do it. I can see the damn building. JC and his "patient" Ray are probably waiting for the elevator right now, which is all good. But if they make it to the ground floor and are standing around with no "ambulance" in sight, it will look pretty suspicious. The traffic begins to surge forward hesitantly with the changing of the light, inertia giving way to the perpetual motion of the city and I'm just focusing on the bumper in front of me. I am not my urgency; it is outside of me like a weather system; I am only energy and drift, and this traffic is a pattern of slowly developing possibilities that ebb and flow with my breathing.

Thank God for my yoga training! My heartbeat is under control and I'm back in front of the building where I dropped JC off before. I park the car and put on the 4-ways. Pop the locks again just to make sure. And then the wheelchair door springs open and out roll the feet of my nemesis, pushed along by JC in a wheelchair marked "Patient Transfer." Ray's head is slumped to the side and he's wearing a Mets hat with an oxygen mask strapped to his face. They come down the ramp to the side of the front steps. JC is decked out in hospital scrubs and actually looks the part. He's tall, so he has that look of unquestionable authority. Stationed behind the reference desk in the London Public Library, with his shoulder length brownish hair, steely blue eyes and nicely trimmed goatee, he is the go-to librarian for the tough Boolean searches or whatever. I get out and walk around to open the curbside door.

"Did the patient behave himself?" I say.

"Tolerably so," he says.

"He's smaller in person than I pictured."

"That's good. He's easier to lift."

JC takes the mask off Ray's face and grabs him under his shoulders. He also looks older than the picture we got off the Internet. He seems to be sleeping peacefully—he's actually unconscious and should be for another few hours. I grab him under his knees and back up toward the back seat of my Honda Civic. I sit down and draw his lower half in with me, positioning him on the seat behind the passenger seat and then we swivel him around so he's sitting upright. While I'm buckling Ray into his seat belt, JC folds up the wheelchair and puts away the mini oxygen tank apparatus. I clamber out of the back seat by the other door.

"Pop the trunk, Watson."

"Shit. Sorry," I say. I fumble with the doors and then find the button. My hands are sweating despite the cold. I approach the trunk to see if I can make myself useful. "Did you get his laptop?"

He holds up the gym bag he had slung over his shoulder. "Check."

"BlackBerry?"

"Cell phone. Check."

"He has his wallet with him?"

"Check."

JC doesn't get impatient with me asking these questions, even though we've been over this about fifty times. He's not the impatient type. While he's packing everything away in the trunk and getting out the things we'll need for the trip, I take a look up and down the sidewalk, searching the faces for questioning looks or recognition. This is exactly the kind of nervous, suspicious behavior I had hoped to avoid. I am supposed to be looking confident and unconcerned, as though I have every reason in the world to be here doing this right now. I get into the driver's seat to wait instead.

I twist around in my seat to get a good look at our prisoner as JC is securing the plastic ties to his wrists and chaining his waist to the seat post. Ray is paunchy, slack-jawed and balding. He has small, pinched features and closely set eyes that are slightly off kilter. Friday must be casual day, because he is wearing navy Dockers and a blue pinstriped button down. His winter coat is a dark green mountain parka that JC has helpfully zipped up for him. The deck shoes aren't going to be great in the snow.

"Didn't he have any boots?" I say.

"None that I could find," says JC, getting in and closing his door. "Probably has underground parking and doesn't care about the snow."

"So, everything is good?"

"Yes. That was strangely easy. I got by the security

desk with our development letter from Ray. I said I was there to meet with him and they told me the floor. And I took his pass card out of his pocket, so I was okay on the way out. You were right, the elevator won't work without a pass card."

"Thought so."

"There was nobody around in the office. The receptionist was just leaving when I got there with my janitor gear on and I cleaned out her garbage first."

"Fantastic. Was she hot?"

"Pretty much. But it was like I was part of the scenery. Nobody takes much notice of a janitor, I guess."

"I had a little incident with a secretarial hotness, too, but that's a story for another day. Are we good to go?"

"Yeah. You want to get some Taco Bell or something?"

My stomach turns over at the thought. "I don't think I could eat. Grab yourself a granola bar out of the glove compartment."

I get turned around to head west on West 57th Street with rush hour in full swing. Luckily it's a straight shot down West 57th to the West Side Highway and then not far to the Lincoln Tunnel and we're out of here. Just have to be patient like Ray, there. We were patient with him all those weeks and months when he wasn't returning our e-mails, phone calls and faxes. Now it's his turn to be patient with us.

Just hearing from a syndicate at all was a dream come true for us. Having grown up on *Peanuts* collections, *Garfield*, *Tintin*, *Asterix & Obelix* and later switching to *Calvin and Hobbes*, *Bloom County* and *Doonesbury*, it seemed completely normal that JC's great artwork and my love of word play should bring us together in the art form that we loved. Part of the fun was dreaming up some new concept every couple of years, writing and drawing about 24 or 36 strips and packaging them up with earnest letters to all the syndicates, always hoping this one will be the one. Our big break. Albeit a break in a dying medium, as JC likes to remind me.

Everything we sent out garnered us form rejection letters and we would move on to the next idea. We were excited when an editor (a Real Editor!) would hand write a note on our form letter. So to actually get a positive response—and a syndication offer! It was unbelievable. "Pinch me" didn't cover it. Hit me in the face with a shovel, knock me down, dance on my stomach in high heels, this can't be real. We were e-mailing back and forth for weeks after we got the phone call. There was an endless number of plans and ideas to share—finding a lawyer, settling the contract, plotting our story arcs, designing our website. We had our heads in the clouds and we weren't coming down.

From: "JC Dubois" <jcdubois76@yeehaw.ca>
To: "Watson Sinclair"
<wsinclair@fullservicebrokers.ca>
Sent: Friday, May 11, 2008 8:09 AM
Subject: Re: Royal Features, baby!

Love the new material! I like where you're going with it. I can totally see the image of James twisted up like a pretzel, but it's a bit early to be talking about our first book collection. I'll send you some roughs to look at by the end of the weekend. Man, this just might work. See you tomorrow!

JC

----- Original Message -----
From: "Watson Sinclair"
<wsinclair@fullservicebrokers.ca>
  To: "JC Dubois" <jcdubois76@yeehaw.ca>
  Sent: Friday, May 11, 2008 6:43 AM
  Subject: Re: Royal Features, baby!

It will all be worth it! Definitely Zen Palace for
Saturday. 6:30 good? And what do you think of
"Pretzel Logic" as the title for the first book collection?
We could have a picture of James all tied up in a yoga
pose and it would also refer to his normal twisted
thought processes when talking to Stella. Anyway,
please find attached seven new scripts to get you
started. I haven't even attended the first class and I'm
already steaming ahead! I'm having so much fun with
this.

Frenchumiwhatsit,
Watson

----- Original Message -----
From: "JC Dubois" <jcdubois76@yeehaw.ca>
  To: "Watson Sinclair"
<wsinclair@fullservicebrokers.ca>
  Sent: Thursday, May 10, 2008 6:43 PM
  Subject: Re: Royal Features, baby!

I'm glad you're feeling so positive about everything.

I don't lack confidence in your abilities; I just question the material we're being given. But the way you put it sounds pretty funny, so that's a good start. Start sending me scripts and I'll start drawing. I feel like I'm going to be working around the clock, even though Ray only wants roughs. Seven strips a week, plus a full time job--tabernac! Let's hope it's all going to be worth it.

Good luck with the yoga class. I like "Yoga for Dummies" as a title, but I'm worried about copyright because of this:

http://www.dummies.com/store/product/Yoga-For-Dummies.productCd-0764551175.html

But I guess Ray will know about that kind of stuff with a whole legal department at his side. Nice to have back-up finally, isn't it? And yes, daydreaming about this has become a big part of my day, too. I bet there are no professional cartoonists that dream about being librarians. :)

I have checked with my better half and we are free on Saturday. Zen Palace, table for four? Let me know. In the meantime, keep your mind on your work or you won't get paid!

A bientot,
JC

----- Original Message -----
From: "Watson Sinclair"
<wsinclair@fullservicebrokers.ca>
To: "JC Dubois" <jcdubois76@yeehaw.ca>
Sent: Thursday, May 10, 2008 7:49 AM
Subject: Re: Royal Features, baby!

Worry not, my man. I can be funny about anything. If you think about it, marriage doesn't seem all that funny, either. To about 50% of people it is a howling misery, I assume. Maybe it is the people who view life as a comedy that survive marriage and those who view it as a tragedy get their divorces in the end.

I already signed up for a yoga class at the gym. The first class is this weekend, so I'll let you know how it goes. Speaking of how it goes, any progress with title ideas? I'm thinking of "The Yoga Master" or "Yoga for Dummies." Have you thought of any others?

This is messing with my head. It's all I can think of. At work, I spend all my time making notes about comic script ideas, ideas for titles, etc. and fantasizing about how I'm going to tell them I'm leaving to be a full-time comic stripper. That will be a sweet day. I was thinking if we get to 3 or 400 papers right away we could probably make a go of it. Then we can get working on another concept, start selling some collections after a year or two and get the website up and running. At home I'm in a daze half the time, babbling on about syndication and reading anniversary collections of other cartoonists to find out about their early days when they were getting started.

Anyway, more on this later. I've got to get to work. We should get together this weekend. You guys free for dinner Friday or Saturday? Talk soon.

Sinclair out!
—

----- Original Message -----
From: "JC Dubois" <jcdubois76@yeehaw.ca>
To: "Watson Sinclair"

<wsinclair@fullservicebrokers.ca>
   Sent: Thursday, May 10, 2008 6:43 AM
   Subject: Re: Royal Features, baby!

Watson.

It's an honour and a privilege to be your creative partner. My head is spinning. It's hard to take this in because I never could believe it. It always seemed like it was just a goof. Something you and I did when we got together because it was fun and we loved comics. I never got the hopeful anticipation you got when we were stuffing the envelopes. I just always thought, there goes 20 bucks in postage that would have got us 2 pitchers at the Roadhouse.

But wow it really happened. At least a development deal happened. I hate to say it, but it's no guarantee yet that we're going to be in newspapers. We still have to prove ourselves to Ray and change our concept by a lot. What do you know about yoga? Is yoga even funny? How are you going to write 50% of these strips about the yoga world and be funny about it? I hope to God that whatever yoga place you go to is dripping with hilarity in every corner, because a lot of our future is riding on it. Also don't hurt yourself. Those pretzel poses look really unnatural.

So yay us. Hope it all comes true. But I'm not quitting my day job and neither should you. I look forward to your phone call, amigo. Until then, I remain...

   Your humble servant,
   JC DuB

   ----- Original Message -----

From: "Watson Sinclair"
<wsinclair@fullservicebrokers.ca>
To: "JC Dubois" <jcdubois76@yeehaw.ca>
Sent: Wednesday, May 09, 2008 7:06 PM
Subject: Royal Features, baby!

Can you believe this? How many people can say their dreams came true on a Wednesday afternoon with a phone call? This is just the beginning of a long road that will lead us to the Promised Land. All our hard work finally paid off. And can I just say that it is a pleasure to be doing this with my best friend. Thanks for agreeing to take this leap of faith and putting in all that work with no promise of a payoff. That's what got us here and that positive thinking and perseverance is going to help get us to the top.

Anyway, here is how I left it with Ray (I call him Ray, now, you know, Ray Bennett, Editorial Director of Royal Features Syndicate? He's my boy, now. We talk on the phone.) today: he's going to send each of us a package of information on what they do for comic feature launches. He likes our concept but wants to change it just slightly to make it something he can sell to newspaper editors. I know, it's going to feel like we're selling out a bit, but I wasn't married (no pun intended) to the idea of James's profession, anyway. He figures that yoga is huge right now and that making James a yoga instructor will be big with the 20-something demographic that newspaper editors are always trying to target. Yes, I'm going to have to take a yoga class! Somebody tell me where to get my spandex, some crystals and the best patchouli incense on the market. Can you picture it? No, me neither. But I'm open to new experiences if it gets us syndicated!

So we have to think of a new name for the strip, pick a logo, think about reserving a web domain for ourselves and go over the contract once Ray gets it ready. Are you ready for some extra work? Maybe you should take a yoga class, too, just for some visual source material. Don't take any pictures, though. That kind of thing will get you booted out. :) I'll call you this weekend and we can go over all this stuff. But for now, just know that I will not rest until we're in 1000 papers and on our way to number 1 in the strip world. Get ready for *Then Comes Marriage 2.0*. All the best of what it was plus the new stuff we have to put in to make it to the show. Look out world, here we come.

Peace.
Watson
--

JC has a whole file folder with our e-mails printed off in the back seat. I have no idea what he intends to do with them. Maybe he wants Ray to read them all to remind him of how we got here.

"So the chloroform worked well, eh?"

"Yeah. Took about a minute of him flailing around with me holding him from behind and him kind of slapping at my arms and head a bit. And grabbing for the phone and whatnot, but his chair was on wheels so I was able to steer him away from danger until he settled down and then went out."

"And then you changed into your hospital gear..."

"Yeah."

"Where did you store the wheelchair during all

this?"

"I just left it by the elevator. Who's going to steal a wheelchair?"

"Good point."

"So I stowed all his stuff in the backpack and then went and got the wheelchair and put him in it. I didn't have room for the janitor uniform, so I put it in his garbage."

"Uh-huh."

"It should be okay."

"I guess. What are they going to do, call Canada and say, 'Got any bearded librarian kidnapper janitors up there who might be harboring a pasty-faced Editorial Director from a doomed artistic endeavor?'"

JC busts out a laugh at that one and it makes me feel better. Talk about pasty-faced, I feel like all the blood has left mine and traveled to my stomach to flush my nerves full of oxygenated anxiety. There is nothing slower than rush hour traffic when you're trying to flee the country. I sneak a peak in the rear-view mirror at our prisoner just in case he might be struggling with his bonds or pulling a knife out of his loafers or something. Nope. His head is lolling towards the window and he's starting to snore. Please God may the weather hold, because I will never be able to sleep if we have to share a hotel room.

"Why is it," I ask JC. "Whenever you are in a hotel and you only get 12 channels so you end up watching some show that you've only ever watched once, that show will always be a rerun and it's the exact one you've seen before?"

JC looks over at me, but I keep my eyes on the road. "Is this a script idea?"

"Maybe."

"Can't we just talk about normal stuff?"

"No, this really happened. You know that show with the twin guys who are divorce lawyers and they're both married to ghost whisperers and they sue the estates of dead husbands for psychically harassing their ex-wives?"

"Shut up. That's not a real show."

My wife thinks we're in New York to attend a comic convention, a necessary lie that she readily believed. I feel bad lying to her because she's my best friend and the love of my life, but I don't think she'd support me in this. And good for her, although she's been wrapped up in it from the beginning. The comic strip idea that started all this came in the most unlikely place: right in front of our noses. As newly married guys, we decided to do a strip about a married couple. Keep it simple, we said. So the great affection I have for my wife's foibles and idiosyncrasies turned into great, funny comic strip ideas. So in a way, it's because of her that I'm here today.

—

For updates on the upcoming publication of *The Launch* and other soon to be announced projects, please sign up for Mark's VIP Mailing List at http://markvictoryoung.com/.